Adrien

CO-WIVES, CO-WIDOWS

translated by Rachael McGill

Dedalus

This book has been selected to receive financial assistance from English PEN's "PEN translates" programme, supported by Arts Council England. English PEN exists to promote literature and our understanding of it, to uphold writers' freedoms around the world, to campaign against the persecution and imprisonment of writers for stating their views, and to promote the friendly co-operation of writers and the exchange of ideas.

Published in the UK by Dedalus Limited
24-26, St Judith's Lane, Sawtry, Cambs, PE28 5XE
email: info@dedalusbooks.com
www.dedalusbooks.com

ISBN printed book 978 1 912868 77 3
ISBN ebook 9781 912868 85 8

Dedalus is distributed in the USA & Canada by SCB Distributors
15608 South New Century Drive, Gardena, CA 90248
email: info@scbdistributors.com   web: www.scbdistributors.com

Dedalus is distributed in Australia by Peribo Pty Ltd
58, Beaumont Road, Mount Kuring-gai, N.S.W. 2080
email: info@peribo.com.au www.peribo.com.au

First published in Mali in 2015
First published by Dedalus in 2021

Printed and bound in the UK by Clays, Elcograf, S.p.A
Typeset by Marie Lane

Dedalus Africa
General Editors: Jethro Soutar
Yovanka Perdigão

CO-WIVES, CO-WIDOWS

Note

The glossary at the end of the book gives the meaning of some of the words and phrases in Sango or French indicated by italics in the text.

The Author

Adrienne Yabouza was born in the Central African Republic in 1965. After fleeing the civil war with her five children in 2013, she gained political asylum in France. She is self-educated, and had a variety of jobs before working as a hairdresser for many years. She now dedicates herself to writing fiction for adults and children, in Sango, Yakoma, Lingala and French.

Co-épouses, co-veuves (*Co-wives, Co-widows*) was published in Mali in 2016 and is her second novel for adults to be published in French.

The Translator

Rachael McGill is a playwright for stage and radio, prose writer and literary translator from French, German, Spanish and Portuguese. Her translation of *The Desert and the Drum* by Mbarek Ould Beyrouk was published by Dedalus in 2018 and was shortlisted for The Oxford-Weidenfeld Translation Prize. Her play *The Lemon Princess* is published by Oberon, as are her translations of the Kerstin Specht plays *Marieluise* (winner of the Gate Theatre/Allied Domecq Translation Award) and *The Time of the Tortoise*.

Her first novel *Fair Trade Heroin* will be published by Dedalus in 2022.

CO-WIVES, CO-WIDOWS

ADRIENNE YABOUZA

TRANSLATED BY RACHAEL MCGILL

WINNER
ENGLISH PEN
AWARD

1

'Who is it?'

'Me!'

'Who's me?'

'Me! Lidou!'

A laugh exploded from behind the door, followed by the word 'coming!'

Ndongo Passy was smoothing cream over her naked body. She grabbed the towel she'd used after her shower and tucked it round her waist. She opened the door. She was caressed by sunlight from head to toe.

'What is it, Lidou?'

He entered the room in silence, pulling the door closed behind him. It took a moment for his eyes to adjust to the dimness. When they did, he gaped at his first wife as if he'd never seen her before. Her nipples, still pert from her shower, pointed in his direction like a challenge.

'What is it Lidou?' Ndongo Passy repeated.

Before he could answer, she let out that laugh again. 'What is this? Have you come straight from my co-wife's room to mine? Don't try to tell me Grekpoubou doesn't know what she's doing!'

'Mother of Gbandagba,' Lidou murmured, 'Come closer. Come over here.'

'I'm here! What do you want?'

He pulled her towards him and began to suck on her breasts as if she was his own mother, not the mother of Gbandagba, his son. He sucked as if he'd been thirsting for those two teats since the beginning of time. After three minutes he stopped, satisfied. Ndongo Passy sat on the edge of the bed.

'It's Sunday, isn't it?' she asked him. 'It's January 24th, isn't it?'

'That's right.'

'Then you have to get out of here now. I need to make myself beautiful. It's election day, remember? I'm on the register, I've got my polling card in my bag. I'm going to go and vote to the best of my abilities, like a good citizen.'

'But do you know how?'

'Yes! My co-wife and I are going down together. We've been discussing this election for some time.'

'What are you going to vote for? Who, I mean?'

'The same as Grekpoubou. We've decided.'

'You didn't consult me!'

'I've got my card, you've got your card. This is every man for himself!'

'But you're not a man, Ndongo Passy. You're my first wife.'

'That's got nothing to do with it. Husband and wife vote separately. That's what democracy is.'

'Who said that?'

Lidou left to let his wife get dressed. In the living room he found Grekpoubou, with whom he'd spent the night. She served him a plate of *yabanda* and a large glass of *kangoya*, then left him alone to eat. She had to make herself beautiful too. It was the first time she'd voted. She was voting for her own future and for that of her four children, who weren't old enough to do it for themselves. Ndongo Passy was voting for herself and for her only child, Gbandagba, who was twelve.

Ndongo Passy wore an indigo suit, her co-wife a long black skirt and a golden yellow blouse. As the two women stepped out into the dusty street, their husband was making himself comfortable in his armchair beneath the shade of the mango tree. 'Safe trip!' he shouted with a chuckle.

Who knows which of the women was the first to complain about the sun. It beat down mercilessly and democratically on all citizens, regardless of gender, ethnicity, religion or age, regardless of whether they planned to vote for the president or to sneak a vote for one of the four opposition candidates into the envelope. The sun, like the mosquito, was pan-sexual and gregarious; every variety of flesh was welcome.

The polling station for the first arrondissement was in the nursery school in Cité Cristophe. It had been open since 7 am. By the time Ndongo Passy and Grekpoubou arrived at 9 am, the queue outside was 25 metres long. A question for the older pupils at the primary school: at a rate of 2.5-2.7 metres of voter per hour, at what time would the two women fulfil their civic duty?

Lidou was in possession of two beautiful wives. He spent two nights with one, the next two with the other, and was never required to choose between them. He preferred to let his two wives go to the polling station alone while he stayed in his courtyard, under the shade of his mango tree, flicking through the Christmas double edition of his French magazine, *Maisons d'aujourd'hui*. He hadn't decided whether to go and vote himself. Making a choice usually meant getting it wrong. This time it was even more devilishly deceptive than usual: five candidates! Like having to choose between five serious illnesses. Mind you, not all serious illnesses packed the same punch; not all were incurable for example. Lidou placed the magazine on his knees for a moment and closed his eyes. Some people said, correctly, that life itself was a mortal illness, that death was a garment everyone would have to put on one day. Maybe that meant he should go and vote; choosing one candidate or the other wasn't as serious as life and death. The world wouldn't end if it turned out he, Lidou, was no better at voting than the next man, even if the next man was as illiterate as a perch in the river.

Lidou's radio was always tuned to *Ndéké Luka*. The music began to work its way under his skin: he could've got up right then and started dancing the *yangbabolo*, alone in the courtyard. Business was good: he was throwing up building after building in the Republic, and he'd carry on for as long as the Congolese and Cameroonian cement lasted. Building houses was as important as voting, more important in fact. At the centre of Lidou's magazine of exclusive new houses built by the French, in France, was a glossy red and white Father Christmas spitting out a speech bubble that said, 'Laying the foundations for a prosperous nation!' Wise words. Santa had certainly earned his status as a prophet, alongside Jesus Christ (amen) and Mohammed (Inch'Allah).

Who better to believe in on election day than Father Christmas and his international prophet friends? Me, thought Lidou. Me and my small business. I'm constructing this country, brick by brick, using nothing but my own graft. I'm a living example of the electoral slogan, 'work, only work'. I should be voting for myself. Come to think of it, I'd probably make an excellent president, but it's not as if I can do everything.

He gazed upwards. A red powder coated the leaves of the mango tree like some sort of leprous plague. Perhaps it would kill the tree. Lidou shuddered, closed his eyes again.

After 3.10 metres of voters, the co-wives had reached an enviable position under the shade of the giant rubber tree that filled the courtyard of the nursery school. A pregnant woman walked the length of the queue to the front. She had priority, as did the old and infirm. If there'd been a pregnant candidate for the presidency, they could all have saved some time by just letting her go first: she'd be elected in the first hour of the first round of voting without even needing to distribute extra polling cards to her friends or pay a magician to make certain ballot boxes appear and certain others disappear.

Time ticked by. 'How are your feet, sister?' Ndongo Passy asked Grekpoubou.

'OK.'

'That's good.'

'But we don't vote with our feet, do we?'

Ndongo Passy burst out laughing. It was probably the

tenth time she'd laughed since she got up that morning. Perhaps it was the laugh that kept her large body, solid but supple, in such good shape.

'You vote with your finger, sister. You press your finger into the ink, just once.'

'Just once, and vote once?'

Standing was becoming difficult for everyone; the woman in front of them had sat down on the ground. Some lucky voters were able to squat with their bottoms on the cement border that ringed the rubber tree. Policemen watched from a few paces. They had a bench, but would clearly have preferred a bed: they slumped, eyes only half open, AK47s slung casually at their feet.

The queue was like a long, lazy, multi-legged *makongo*. But, against all expectations, and without ever getting any shorter, it moved forward. Ndongo Passy and Grekpoubou were now not far from the door to the office, a location as sought-after as Ali Baba's cave.

Two white men appeared with cards hanging from blue cords around their necks. They were from the EU, an organisation that preferred presidents to seek re-election by consulting their people. These were the kind of EUs who might say, 'This election could do with a bit more salt, but it's basically acceptable'. As they entered the building, one said to the other, 'This crowd reminds me of queuing for a Michel Sardou concert at the Olympia as a kid.'

The other, a slightly classier type, smiled and said, 'It reminds me of the Tutankhamun exhibition.'

An old woman in the queue, dried out by that morning's and yesterday's sun, murmured to herself, 'At the end of

14

patience is heaven.'

Five minutes later, the two whites mandated by the Union of Whites came back out and climbed into their 4x4, the air-con reminding them of their skiing holidays (in the French Alps in one case, the Bavarian in the other).

What was supposed to occur finally did occur: Ndongo Passy and Grekpoubou reached the office. They took their time exercising their democratic duty: voting for the first time feels no less momentous than being elected president for the first time. Ndongo Passy savoured the sense of importance of sliding her ballot paper into the box, despite the looks from the officials, who all seemed to have been struck by toothache.

As soon as they got outside, Grekpoubou whispered, 'In the booth I went in, someone had done a piss!'

'No!'

'Yes!'

'I suppose they just couldn't hold on any longer.'

Lidou lounged in the dusty street at the door of his compound. He was hungry. It was high time his wives came back. He'd read his French magazine twice. He'd chosen a design for a family home he could adapt to the local market and start building immediately. A whole series of them, perhaps.

The two women came towards him, their steps in time. As Lidou watched them approach, each as beautiful as the other, he felt his power. He filled his lungs with the hot, dry city air. He had these women, he had his truck, he had his building sites. His status was high. He wasn't a man who had to stand on tiptoe to be noticed. He forgot for a moment that he was only a human being, that he only had two legs, that two legs might not really be enough to chase two hares at the same time.

'There you are! What's going on down there?'

'There's a crowd,' said Ndongo Passy. 'Democracy must've been handing out thousand franc notes to people to come and vote.'

'You took a long time!'

'Yes, and we only voted once, with one finger, not ten times with ten fingers.'

'Are you going to go and do democracy or not, Lidou?' Grekpoubou asked.

'Hmm… I'm hungry. My wives are using their mouths to chatter while my mouth's hungry. Do you catch my drift?'

'We're all about to eat.'

Grekpoubou's daughters and Yaché had already prepared lunch. If he'd wanted to, Lidou could've gone and filled his stomach. The big pot sitting on the hearth stones in the outdoor kitchen didn't have a blackened bottom for nothing. Three pairs of eyes had been fixed on it for hours, as if their owners were afraid it might sprout wings and fly away. Those six eyes belonged to a girl of twelve, a girl of eight and a girl of six: twenty six years in total, the perfect age for a cook. The girls had chopped up the manioc leaves, boiled them, pounded and pounded them in the mortar, then added the peanut paste, the oil, the salt and the smoked fish. They'd done their job to perfection.

Grekpoubou and Ndongo Passy disappeared into their bedrooms and re-emerged in loose *kaba* dresses and indoor mules. They took their seats on the small wooden stools next to Lidou and the boys under the mango tree. The girls placed the big serving dish on a rattan mat. Election day was a day for celebration. Grekpoubou served everyone. Lidou was the first

16

to put his fingers, untouched by the voting ink, to his plate, then to his mouth. Soon all the other hands dived in. The food was very good.

The dish was large: after everyone had been served, there was still enough left for a passing neighbour or friend. Which was lucky, because Lidou's cousin Zouaboua was passing.

'Sit down, Zouaboua, make yourself at home. There's enough shade for everyone, and plenty of food to go round.'

'Thank you, I will.'

He took his seat without further ado. They all polished off the *yabanda* together without another word. Tangani, the youngest child, went without being asked to fetch a basin of water, soap and a cloth so everyone could wash their hands.

Ndongo Passy presented the inked finger of a proud citizen and said, 'Is this ink indelible? Or is it just terrible?'

'Indelible?' Where had she got that white man's word? Lidou didn't even know what it meant. She explained, and everyone laughed. She shook her finger as she added, 'We'll know when the results are out. If my candidate wins, it was indelible; if another one wins, it was terrible.'

'Who wants *kangoya*?' asked Lidou. 'Who's for beer? Who's for *bili-bili*?'

Everyone picked one, except the children, who had gone to watch '*Capitaine Biceps*' on *Télétoon*.

After drinking two gourds of *bili-bili*, Lidou wouldn't have said no to popping inside with Ndongo Passy for a round of two person push-ups. He stretched, looked at them all and said, 'Hey, Zouaboua, have you already voted out there in Poto Poto?'

'Yes, I went when it opened.'

'You did?'

'It opened an hour late, though.'

'I know who you voted for.'

'Do you?'

'You voted for the current president. You always vote for the current president. Should I go and vote too, then? Who should I vote for? Fine. I'll go. Perhaps I'll do it better than all of you did.'

'Who or what are you going to vote for?' asked Grekpoubou.

'I think I'll vote for all five, so whoever wins makes me Minister for Newbuild Housing.'

Everyone laughed. Lidou stood up. Zouaboua did the same. Grekpoubou called after them, 'Watch out in the booth. Someone pissed in one of them this morning!'

Ndongo Passy and Grekpoubou took up their usual places in the street, one on either side of the compound gate. Ndongo Passy had peanuts and a mini mountain of manioc in a washing up basin, while Grekpoubou sold small dresses for girls and small shorts for boys. She'd sewn them herself on an old pedal-operated Singer she'd got from her mother.

A gentle breeze blew, perhaps just to provide a coating of colour to the mangoes that were still too green.

2

Had he burned himself out in his eagerness to succeed? It was the sort of thing a traditional medicine man would probably say – something to the effect that Lidou had been sprinting for the future instead of strolling through the present. But forty nine wasn't old. He was still fit. He wouldn't be building houses today if he hadn't built himself first, been out in the world laying his foundations while his classmates were still chewing on their pencils in the sixth form. Perhaps that was it: those years he'd worked himself hard while he was still growing were weighing on him now.

The night before, with Grekpoubou, he'd been next to useless. They'd washed each other playfully with lukewarm water, given each other's backs a scratch. When they lay down together he'd felt his desire for her; in his mouth, in his hands, and elsewhere.

Lidou sat in front of his breakfast plate of *ngoundja,* taking stock. He'd always been a star striker with both Grekpoubou and Ndongo Passy. Lately it seemed he was losing his touch. This was a sombre morning, despite the sun laughing in the sky. Had the time come to pay through the nose for some imported white man's remedy?

He pondered further. He'd practically given up smoking, he only accepted every other beer these days and he only ever touched *kangoya* or *bili-bili* on Sundays, or mostly only then. He ate hearty portions of *gozo* and rice. When his troubles had first started, he'd tried a regimen of the local *afro*disiacs — kola nut, chinchona bark and ginger — for a fortnight. One week he'd swallowed a whole packet of *Tromole* from the Sudanese market. None of it had made any difference. It had been getting worse, until the night before, his worst performance yet, when the goal had eluded him completely. Grekpoubou had done her best: she'd looked as delicate as a dry season dragonfly, a belt of red and yellow beads swinging round her hips. She was like a league champion representing Africa in the night-time game.

Lidou made a decision: on the way to the building site he'd stop off to see his good friend who worked at the chemist on the Avenue of the Fiftieth Anniversary of Independence. He'd get some of the blue miracle pills, or something rainbow-coloured and even stronger, just as long as it said 'made in France' on it. Those pills were highly effective: you only had to look at all the old Bangui crocodiles still in the game to see that. The whites could perform those kinds of miracles; they'd been doing it since colonial times, and even before that, right back to Mary, the Mother of God, who'd had a child without sinning.

The sun beat down as unrelentingly as ever. It had, Lidou mused, been burning the earth and the sky since the time of Emperor Bokassa I, since before the coronation; it had probably been lashing the planet with its rays even before human beings were separated into blacks, whites, yellows and reds, before anyone decided which group should become the slaves and which the masters.

He pushed his Raybans, purchased in Dubai, up his nose. How contemplative he was that morning, musing on the working of miracles and the power of the sun, deeper in his thoughts than a relative trying to draft an insincere eulogy for a bigwig's funeral.

When Lidou's car left the compound, Grekpoubou and Ndongo Passy were already in their places at the front gate, selling their wares. They got not so much as a wave from their husband. They exchanged a questioning glance.

'What's up with him this morning?' asked Ndongo Passy.

Grekpoubou was silent; she worried she might be partly to blame. Little Yaché ran up to them. She was the child, of the child, of an aunt of Lidou's. She'd left her village to come to the city and help the co-wives with the house.

'Has he left?'

'Yes. What did you want?'

'This.'

'What's 'this'?'

'It's for Lidou. Zouaboua brought it this morning, when I was preparing the fire.'

'What did he say?'

He said, 'It's urgent, it's for Lidou, for his work.'

'This' was a bottle that had once contained a litre and a

half of Ubangi river water and was now filled with a pinkish liquid. 'Give that here,' said Ndongo Passy. 'Let me see it.'

Yaché passed it over. Ndongo Passy opened the bottle and sniffed the contents.

'It doesn't smell as good as *J'adore* by Dior. It doesn't even smell as good as whisky.'

She returned the bottle to Yaché. 'You can give it to him tonight when he gets home. Just say Zouaboua came too late this morning.'

The co-wives sat in silence. Ndongo Passy began to absently caress the mound of manioc in her basin, transforming it into a small, pointed hill. The children were at school, Lidou at work. Hopefully some chatty friends would turn up soon with their own basins of produce to sell. Then they could all have a gossip, insult their husbands, perhaps exchange some observations on democracy, which still hadn't delivered the election results, though the president of the Independent Electoral Commission had already bought himself a speedy new 4x4.

'Lidou, brother, how are you?'

'Fifty percent.'

'What? What does that mean?'

'It means I'm half well. I'm OK in the day time, when I'm only thinking about work, but not at night, when I'd rather be thinking about the fifth or sixth or seventh heaven.'

'I see.'

'You're my soul brother, Djozo, and you're a pharmacist. You know I've got two wives at home. You have to help me.'

Djozo nodded. He took Lidou by the arm and led him into

a corner where they could talk in private.

'Do you have air-conditioning in your bedroom?'

'Of course; everyone does!'

'That could be it. It's a well-known fact that cold can destroy sensation.'

'But I've always had the air-con. And Ndongo Passy and Grekpoubou are hot. They're like two chilli peppers!'

'If it's not the air-con, then…'

'Then what?'

'Then it's bad. But I know what you need. Have you got a strong heart?'

'My heart's like a diamond, Djozo, strong and pure!'

'Good. So, to help you to achieve the desired… eruption, I'm going to give you the newest pills I have. These things cut your age in half. But please remember: you must only take one dose, just before you need to perform. If you want to get back in the saddle again in the middle of the night, or the next morning, don't take another pill, that's too much.'

'Are they expensive?'

'Very expensive, and then some. But I think you can afford them, just as all the MPs and the president can.'

'Well, give them to me, Djozo, but give me a good price.'

'To be able to play on into extra time with your wives, Lidou, no price is too high!'

At the site, Lidou's houses were taking shape: his flagship project was almost complete. He donned the professional builder's helmet that he was never without during work hours and entered his red-brick world. He loved the smell of cement: its odour had hung around his body since the first hairs had sprouted from his chin. He checked the wooden scaffolding was secure, then agile as a gorilla, he clambered up to survey the first floor. The whole site was spread out at his feet. He wanted to cry with joy at his brilliance as a builder, to plant his flag up there like a mountaineer at the summit of Everest.

He left his workers to their back-breaking labour and set off for a business meeting in PK 5.[1] He tuned to *Radio Bangui*, where the IEC president was finally announcing the election results. He was sparing with his words, drip-dripping the figures one polling station at a time. It was a tedious process, but there was no need to be as crafty as a *makako* to understand that the candidate who'd been in the lead throughout the race would be declared the winner in the first round, as expected.

Lidou's problem gnawed at him like toothache. It was not yet midday when he appeared back at the compound. He ignored his wives and went into the living room. He sat down and unfolded the instruction sheet for the miracle pill, *Cialis*. The instructions appeared in English, then Arabic, then gobbledygook, then, thank God, French. Speakers of every language could experience this betrayal by their bodies then. There was something reassuring about that, in a world in which by far the largest share of life's problems seemed to be reserved for people whose skin colour was black.

Lidou read and re-read the information for ignorant beginners explaining that it was important to adhere to the instructions and not to give the medicine to children. At this point, Yaché came in with the bottle from Zouaboua. Lidou listened to her and smiled. With the miracle medicine from the

---

[1] The abbreviation PK is used to denote areas in Bangui according to their distance in kilometres from the centre.

whites plus the pink native potion in the bottle, he'd be able to keep playing well into extra time.

He swallowed the first pill and a quarter of the pink potion. Then he went and stashed his secret substances in his lockable desk drawer, next to his accounts. Ndongo Passy came in.

'What are you doing, Lidou?'

'Nothing. I'm about to take a nap.'

'Don't you want something to eat?'

'No, I'm fine, I'll eat this evening. What are you doing?'

'Just living my life. A woman does get a spare moment in her life now and again.'

'Would you come in a little while and give my back a rub?'

'Before tonight, you mean?'

'Why not? You got the dinner ready this morning, didn't you?'

'Yes. But who'll do the washing? Who'll clean the living room?'

Lidou went to his bedroom. He half opened the window and the door, so the air could circulate. He'd taken the best possible remedy, but he still felt suspicious of the air-con.

The big eyelid of night had closed over Bangui. The electric lighting scattered across the city was impressive to behold, especially the line that passed by the paediatric hospital and ended at the presidential palace. Power cuts were unknown in that part of town, only water shortages now and then. Lidou's compound was ideally situated: his courtyard was proudly illuminated by a neon strip. The mattress in Ndongo Passy's room was very good. She'd bought it in Ryan with the money she'd saved from three years of selling manioc; 'very-too-expensive', she'd called it. Lidou lay on his back on her bed, hands behind his head. A small lamp provided just the right amount of illumination. Ndongo Passy would be with him soon. Lidou waited, listening to the water running in the shower. That water was caressing every part of his first wife's body, without even asking permission. He'd tuned to *Radio France Internationale*, to see if the rest of the world might mention their country, instead of all the Arab countries where things were always going from bad to worse. But they were playing '*La Maladie d'amour*': 'it runs, it runs, the disease of love...' Lidou loved that song. Songs like that, or like '*Cadenas*' by Fally Ipupa, could bring tears to his eyes. Love was a better system than democracy. It could go wrong and cause suffering of course, just as democracy could, but when it worked well, it was the best political regime in the world.

The bedroom door opened. Ndongo Passy, never shy of being seen, switched on the ceiling light and said, 'How many eyes do you have, Lidou?'

'What, me?'

'It's you I'm talking to, not the cockroaches or the mosquitoes!'

'I've got two eyes.'

'And is that enough to see all of me?'

'You think I might need another eye or two?'

'You might.'

'But I can see you with my mouth as well, and with all the fingers on my hands.'

'Ah. Have a look, then.'

She removed her towel. Lidou's first wife was beautiful;

her beauty continued to ripen with every year. All the hills and valleys of her body were inviting. She approached and kneeled on the bed. It was then that Lidou discovered his name written on her skin. He was speechless for a moment. Those letters, there, in that place; they were like a personal invitation to open the secret door that led to wonderland. Ndongo Passy bowed her head, not in humility but to indicate the neatly-shaven triangle beneath her belly. She got up, switched off the main light, and came into her husband's arms.

Lidou felt his spirits revive. The power of one or other, or both, of the medicines coursed through him. 'Why did you do that?' he asked her.

'For you, Lidou.'

Lidou had no more wish to exchange sweet words. He pinned his wife to the sheet. She said, 'Hey, what's the rush? Have you got diarrhoea or something?'

Lidou made no reply. He came inside her, then rolled her on top of him, then rolled on top of her again. She managed to say, 'What are you doing?'

'We have to fly together, now! Fly to the top of the sky!'

He wanted to cry out, 'Mother,' but the mother of Gbandagba cried out first. A jumble of sounds spilled from both their mouths. Lidou gasped. Ndongo Passy returned to the world, not flayed alive after all, as her shrieks might have suggested. She murmured 'Lidou, Lidou,' before stretching out beside him.

They lay there for several minutes without saying a word. The room seemed to be moving, carrying them far away, to somewhere at the centre of the earth.

Ndongo Passy got up and pressed the switch that started

the rumble of the air-con. Lidou snapped back to reality. He jumped up and cried, 'No! Not that!'

'But cool air will do our bodies good!'

'Don't say that. Air-con is bad for playing dominoes at night.'

'Since when?'

'Since.'

The night lasted, as nights always do, until morning. Ndongo Passy got very little sleep. It was as if Lidou wanted to play every round in the domino world championship before dawn. She got up and staggered to the shower, where the cool water revived her exhausted flesh. Fortunately she only had to re-heat the *ngoundja* from the night before for the morning meal.

Little Yaché helped get the children ready for school. Grekpoubou was as invisible as the wind.

3

Lidou carried on exhausting his wives for two nights, two more nights, then two more. That didn't stop him spending two days, two more days, then two more working from dawn until dusk moving things along on his building sites. On Saturday morning, he finally took a break. He ate a white man's breakfast of bread and jam, followed by bread with butter and wild forest honey stolen by the Pygmies from the bees. Yaché served him two large cups of coffee. Life was good. Rain had washed the red dust from the leaves of the trees; they looked shiny, as if they'd been varnished.

Above Lidou's head, the many leaves of the mango tree provided shelter from the sky. The first heat of the day was agreeable.

He stretched out in his artisan *nguèndè* chair, his feet resting on a wooden footstool, savouring the morning's warmth. He gazed at the mango tree above him and thought, 'That fruit hanging there is the tree's balls. The mango is a tree with serious balls. '

He tuned to *Radio Ndéké Luka*. His wives had gone to the French mass at the Cathedral of the Immaculate Conception. He'd said to them a thousand times, 'I'll listen to the mass in French, in Sango, or in Chinese, the day they give me a cathedral to build. I could build a cathedral, taller than all the trees in the forest!' He'd said the same thing about the mosque. Gothic architecture, Roman, Sudanese, Muslim Arab... none of it intimidated him. His words on religion were meant in jest, of course; all the various Good Lords understood that, only perhaps taking them the wrong way on a bad day, when a wife was being mean, or a fish bone had got stuck.

For some reason, or no reason at all, Lidou felt a sudden pain in his chest. It was a burning kind of pain. It began to get worse. It travelled to his left arm. He dropped his radio on the floor. He tried to take deep breaths of the courtyard air, to flush away the pain, but the pain kept getting worse. He was panting now, his face contorted. He tried to call out, but his voice was weak and was drowned out by Flavour singing his hit song '*Ashewo*', one time too many, on the radio. The four children Lidou had made with Grekpoubou were elsewhere, the son he'd given Ndongo Passy was probably still in bed. Yaché had gone out, to get her hair braided, perhaps.

Lidou never got to know the content of the sermon his wives heard at the cathedral that day; a pity, because the priest's words were apt: he declared, with the conviction of a slam poet or a travel agent, that life was easier in the other world than in this one; that in the other world breathing came more easily. Lidou never got to know the final election result; the constitutional court had yet to pronounce when the pain attacked him. Nobody came, and after a short period of intense suffering, Lidou set out alone for the house of his ancestors.

A dead man is no trouble to anyone. Lidou remained where he was, one dead leg resting on the footstool, two dead arms folded across a dead chest, a dead head presiding over it all with wide open eyes. His *nguèndè* chair served as a provisional coffin.

A little less than half an hour later, Gbandagba walked into the courtyard. He wondered why his father was sleeping, whether he might be drunk. He approached, puzzled. His father was not an abuser of beer or *kangoya,* and it was still morning. Even the worst drunks, in town or in the bush, were fairly well behaved in the morning.

'What is it, Dad?'

Lidou made no reply. He wasn't sulking; he was just one of those dead people who doesn't speak.

Gbandagba repeated his question, reaching out to touch his father's hand. The hand was still warm, but Gbandagba noticed a sort of paralysis in the fingers. A few seconds later, he understood. He dropped the length of bamboo he'd just been using as a fishing rod, and the little bag around his neck containing the two *kessés* and three *ngoros* he'd caught in the Oubangui river. He cried out, 'Dad!' and ran into the house, still shouting 'Dad! Dad! Dad!'

There was no living being around to hear him. Gbandagba was frightened. Were his mothers and his brother and sisters dead somewhere too? He didn't try to answer the question he'd asked himself, but ran out of the compound, to the house of the neighbour, Georgine.

Georgine was sitting with both her hands in a basin of washing.

'Quick, he's dead! They're dead!'

'Who's dead?'

'Dad! There…'

'What? And the others?'

The boy was panic-stricken. Georgine hoisted herself to her feet. Despite her considerable weight, she attempted to run behind Gbandagba, who'd taken her hand and was pulling her along.

There was no need to question Lidou: Georgine could see at first glance that he was no longer with the living. A quick-thinking woman, she grabbed her phone, which she always kept tucked cosy inside her bra, and called Ndongo Passy. She said to herself, the dead man, the mango tree and Gbandagba, 'I hope there isn't a problem with the network!'

By some post-mass miracle, she reached Ndongo Passy on the first try.

'Georgine, what is it? Has something happened?'

Georgine's throat was dry. How to express to a wife that she'd just become a widow? It was worse for a woman to say that to another woman than for the president of the IEC to announce the election results to the entire assembled opposition. Georgine tripped over her words, and ended up saying, 'Lidou… under the mango tree… Gbandagba… he'd got back from fishing…'

'What are you saying, sister? Explain yourself!'

'You need to come back to the house, now!'

'What's happened? Is the house on fire?'

'Come!'

Georgine hung up. Ndongo Passy and Grekpoubou were both under their umbrellas to protect them from the sun. Ndongo Passy told her co-wife, 'It was Georgine. I don't know what she was saying, she was speaking all back to front.'

'What?'

'Speaking in code. I don't understand. Well, we'll be there soon.'

It was true: the walk from the cathedral to the house took no more than ten minutes. The co-wives tried to walk more quickly, but their ankle-length *pagnes* restricted their steps.

Georgine was a mother. As soon as she'd alerted the other neighbours, she took hold of Gbandagba, pressed him against her large chest and began to rock him. They were standing like that at the door of the compound when Lidou's wives arrived. They understood immediately that it was bad.

'What's happened?'

'Oh, my sisters, there's been a loss!'

'Who is it?'

Ndongo Passy had guessed. The tears on the faces of all the neighbours could only mean that a great baobab tree had been uprooted. Georgine let go of Gbandagba, took the hands of the two women and murmured, 'Lidou is dead.'

For a moment they didn't speak or react. It was as if the information was false. When they left for mass, Lidou had waved goodbye. He'd had shaving foam on his face. They'd teased him; Grekpoubou had shouted, 'I don't fancy you when you dress up like a white man!' Then suddenly it was as if the same spring had uncoiled inside both women: they rushed towards Lidou's corpse, which had been laid down on a mat. Strangely, someone had placed the small radio next to Lidou's ear. Switched off, it now seemed dead too.

The co-wives fell to their knees, one on either side of the corpse, and started to cry, to wail, to beat their fists on the ground. The neighbours stepped back to allow the women space for their grief. Grekpoubou rolled herself into a ball on the ground. She lost all control of her body and her mind. She no longer knew where she was, only that she wanted to escape the world completely, to find some other place where she could hide herself away, all alone, to recover. Ndongo Passy walked round and round the body, then went round it again on her knees, then on her bottom, then on all fours. It was a strange sort of dance known only to her, or perhaps only to her limbs, acting of their own volition. Neither Grekpoubou nor Ndongo Passy asked themselves which wife, the first or the second, might feel the greater pain.

To help divide up the suffering, the neighbour women all began to cry too. The courtyard was filled with sobs, chants, and comings and goings that could be heard from all around. Dogs began to bark. Those who had eyes for such things noticed that the still-green mangoes were swaying, doing their own dance in recognition of the pain of those who'd just been reminded, that in the end everyone turns to dust.

It was the red dust of the courtyard that was floating up to the sky as Zouaboua arrived. He understood immediately what had happened. Perhaps he'd left his eyes in the compound after his last visit.

The neighbours had moved the corpse into the living room. The co-wives were sitting immobile on the steps up to the house. Zouaboua approached them and touched their shoulders. He said, 'Be strong.'

Yaché came back from the hairdresser, braided and beautiful. She was ready to make herself useful for days and nights if necessary, but her usual workplace, the courtyard, had been occupied. She didn't know where to put herself. She sat down, like a third grieving widow, next to Grekpoubou and Ndongo Passy. Grekpoubou's children returned from the market and placed the food they'd bought beneath the mango tree. They cried and were given little attention. The courtyard and the living room teemed like termite mounds under construction. More and more neighbours arrived, then Zouaboua, who'd disappeared, was back again like a jolt, entering the courtyard behind the wheel of a double-cabined 4x4 pick-up, blaring his horn loudly enough to wake Lidou from his peaceful death. He stopped the car next to the widows, got out and called to Georgine, 'Bring Lidou here. I'll take him to the community hospital.'

'But Lidou's entirely dead! What can the hospital do for him?'

'He's dead, yes, so I want his body examined. My brother was fine when I saw him yesterday.'

He'd spoken with the authority of someone who'd long been in a position to be generous. Georgine obeyed. She and four other women and one man laid Lidou down in the bed of Zouaboua's truck. Like all fresh corpses, Lidou made no protest. Zouaboua asked Georgine to get into the cabin and accompany him to the hospital. He ordered a male neighbour to sit in the back with the body.

Before they set off, Zouaboua ran back into the house and

locked the doors to the widow's bedrooms, Lidou's bedroom, Lidou's office and the hallway. He put all the keys in his pocket and said to the widows, 'The house is closed. Entry is forbidden. You can wait in the living room.'

Ndongo Passy revived with a start. She jumped to her feet and walked barefoot after Zouaboua. She'd just grasped what he was trying to do. Her head turned stormy, like a sky at the start of the dry season, zebra-striped with flashes that promised thunder and tornadoes. She grabbed hold of Zouaboua, or rather of the head of the Pope that adorned his shirt, and started to shake him. She shouted, 'This thief wants to steal my husband! He's stealing from me and my co-wife!'As her mouth continued to shout, her sharp fingernails began to scratch. Zouaboua, though solid, began to find himself in difficulty: soon he was bleeding from a scratch on his cheek and another on his chest. It was only then that neighbours moved to separate them. Zouaboua shouted, 'You, Ndongo Passy, are a witch!'

'What did you say?'

'A witch! You had that child there, your son, in your belly for fifty-seven months before he was born. I know it! It was you who killed Lidou!'

Wild with rage, Ndongo Passy spat as she shouted, 'I'm an honourable woman! You will not silence me! You're as bad as a *Banyamuléngué*, as bad as a *Zakawa*, you have no respect for life or for death, you're a dirty, low-down killer!'

Furious and humiliated, Zouaboua climbed into his 4x4 and quickly started it up, hurtling out of the courtyard so quickly that Georgine, beside him in the cabin, nearly died of fright, as did Mbilakoué, in the back with the body.

Zouaboua steered with one hand, used the other to wipe the blood from his cheek and chest. The chaos of the city's roads didn't distract him. He pressed his phone to his ear and called Lidou's older sister Songowali. He asked her to meet him at the hospital. Their conversation would have lasted longer; he would have poured all his rage and hate for Ndongo Passy into Songowali's ear, if the network hadn't shut him up by cutting out. A moment later, when his signal returned, he made a call to a doctor at the hospital whom he knew well.

The dead man enjoyed blue sky and sunshine for the last time perhaps. It was very hot in Bangui that day; in the evening, under cover of darkness, the clouds would probably slip down from the hill to the river and piss joyfully all over the town. The second rainy season of the mango harvest wasn't far off: the fruits would soon turn ripe and yellow, showing everyone that sometimes time could move slowly, sometimes it could hurry by.

Mbilakoué, the neighbour, peeked at the body out of the corner of his eye. Lidou looked large and beautiful. His cheeks and his head were closely shaven and he had the serious air of a believer who'd closed his eyes to better communicate with a prophet. Just before they reached the hospital, Mbilakoué dared to look full at Lidou for the last time. Perhaps, he thought, they were taking him to the hospital morgue so he could take part in a competition for the most beautiful dead body.

He chuckled at his idea. A bit of money, maybe even a lot of money, could be made from that idea! It was already far too expensive to bury your deceased family members well, but this was Africa: Africa was always ready for new ideas for mopping up money from people who didn't have it but could borrow it. It wasn't just whites who could play at borrowing cash. The competition for most beautiful dead body, the annual Miss Dead, would have an entry fee, of course. He would submit the idea to the Ministry of New Ideas before anyone could steal it from him. There was a small risk mind you, that someone might kill a wife, a husband or a child who didn't have much to offer while alive, but might make a perfect dead body.

Zouaboua stopped the car. They'd arrived, and he knew what he had to do. He'd worked for so many years facilitating the lies of the powerful that he knew exactly who to speak to in any public or private service. He knew the code, the great poem passed down through the oral tradition, that prescribed which small note should be slipped into the pocket of which small person, and what quantity of large notes should be placed in a large envelope for a larger person.

4

She waited in the accident and emergency department, beneath a large and elegantly-expressed notice from the National Anti-Corruption Committee. The notice was ignored by everyone. Some joker with a PhD in contemporary literature had scrolled at the bottom, 'Read from top to bottom or left to right. Dada speaks!' Songowali waited. The dead are in no rush: being dead lasts for life, at the very least. No matter where you are in the world, death will be boundless. You might die all over again; of boredom.

The porters stood, in manioc-white shirts, as proud as astronauts about to blast off for the stars, waiting for their client. They were engaged in one of their on-going debates, about women who lighten their skin. The older of the two said, 'It's racist to want to be as white as a medical swab!' The other one giggled like a pack of spotted hyenas and said, 'A black woman can never be white; those creams just turn her yellow like a papaya!' He was about to say more, but Zouaboua had got off the phone and was gesturing towards them.

'We're needed. You betting on a male or a female client?'

'Male. A hippopotamus who's had too much palm wine.' They both laughed.

'Come, quickly!' shouted Zouaboua. 'My brother in the back of the truck is dead.'

The porters established that Lidou was indeed one hundred percent dead. The older of the two muttered, 'OK, we'll take care of him, there's no hurry.' They put the body on a trolley and pushed it a little way down the corridor.

Songowali exchanged three words with Zouaboua, passed him a brown envelope, then disappeared into the hospital's labyrinth of corridors. When she returned a minute later, she had a doctor with her. You could tell he was a doctor because he wore a blue tunic and a stethoscope round his neck like a necklace. Also because his badge read *Doctor Émile Ngando*. Dr Ngando recognised Zouaboua. He said, 'Hello brother! What can I do for you?'

'It's my cousin, as I said. He dropped dead. Before he died, he was alive. Very alive, you might say. I visited him yesterday, and he was fine.'

'That's how it goes, my brother: one day you're here, the next day death has snuffed you out. Death is invincible.'

'Well, yes. But in this case, he was poisoned.'

'Really?'

'Yes.'

'By whom? And why?'

'Those things are unknown. Except that I know them.'

40

'What do you know?'

'His wives did it, because he'd got rich enough.'

The doctor gazed down at the body, still waiting on its trolley. He said to the porters, 'Put him in my consulting room for a moment. You know where that is; it's marked *Doctor Émile Ngando.*'

'We know.'

The trolley glided down the corridor like skis moving through snow. Songowali and Zouaboua walked behind it, sandwiching the doctor between them. Zouaboua said, 'We won the first round outright in the 9th arrondissement, with a decent lead. That's one more good representative.'

'True, and we'll get a lot more in the second round.'

They'd lost sight of the porters and the dead man, but as they turned a corner they saw them entering a consulting room intended for the living. Zouaboua was no magician, but he managed to make the brown envelope appear from his pocket. He handed it to the doctor, who barely glanced at it before slipping it beneath his shirt and into one of his own trouser pockets, appreciating its thickness between his index finger and thumb.

Songowali and Zouaboua followed their friend Émile Ngando through the waiting room, where a woman with a goitre sat next to a man with a goitre, and a dozen other patients patiently tolerated their pain, and into the consulting room.

Once they were alone with the dead man, Zouaboua pointed at Lidou and said, 'Yes, poisoned, poor man.'

Émile Ngando sat down behind his desk and assessed the dead man from there. He took a nice, clean sheet of white paper, on to which he placed a stamp, transforming it into official hospital stationery. He mumbled, 'Right, yes… by all accounts poisoned, no mistake.'

He took a beautiful fountain pen from his shirt pocket and wrote with his right hand, in a script not much better than a centipede would have managed:

I the undersigned, Doctor Émile Ngando, serving at the community hospital on Saturday 5th February 2011, declare that I examined Mr Faustin Lidou on his arrival at the accident and emergency department.

I confirmed the death of the above-named and proceeded to note unusual pigmentation on the skin of his face, arms and abdomen, leading me to conclude that his death was not the result of natural causes.

I consider the probability of death by poisoning to be very high. The physical signs, in addition to testimonies collected from relatives of the deceased (his older sister Songowali and his cousin Zouaboua) leave no room for doubt.

Serving all legal intents and purposes, here at the community hospital of Bangui.

He dated his lie and added a magisterial signature as if he was the treasurer of the United States endorsing the thousand dollar bill. He re-read his text before looking up at Zouaboua and Songowali, who smiled.

The office was starting to feel stuffy. The doctor stood up, switched on the air-con with his right hand, and with his left, passed an envelope containing the precious signed declaration to Zouaboua. There was nothing to add, except a little more electoral small talk as they said their goodbyes.

'We'll have a nice majority in the assembly.'

'I think so, and the new deputies representing us at *EMCCA* will understand us even better than the previous ones.'

To conclude, Ngando said, 'I'll have the body taken to the morgue. It will be accessible to the family immediately.'

Back behind the wheel on the Road of the Martyrs, Songowali beside him, Zouaboua smiled. Georgine and the other neighbour had already taken a taxi back home. Zouaboua said, 'Can you see to the printing of the funeral programme, Songowali? The sooner the better.'

'I can,' said Songowali.

'I'll go to the radio station and have them announce Lidou's death later today. Then I'll order a nice coffin. As soon as you get back to our compound, decide on the burial location with the family. We'll need to get hold of the youth orchestra from church.'

They drove for half a minute without speaking. Then Songowali asked tentatively, almost timidly, 'And the widows?'

Zouaboua laughed. 'I'll deal with them too. They'll inherit the ripe mangoes, nothing more.'

Back at the widows' compound, chaos reigned. Lidou had been well-liked in the area, but Ndongo Passy was loved. When someone needed an iron, she'd lend them hers; when a child or an adult needed a paracetamol, she'd provide it; when a young girl got her period for the first time, it was Ndongo Passy who paid for her sanitary towels and explained what could result from passion without precautions. She was the mother of the neighbourhood, and more beautiful in most people's opinion than all the saints in the church, though it might be sacrilege to say so out loud.

Grekpoubou was a simple person, but she too never forgot to be kind. She was honest and entirely without spite. Lidou had struck lucky with those two (and they were good cooks and passionate in bed as well!). He was less lucky to have dropped dead just when he had it all: his own compound, his little construction company, his van, his nearly-new car and two much-admired women.

In the courtyard there was fish with rice, *gozo,* smoked meat, juice and fresh water. It was impossible to know who'd brought it; it was undocumented food, without papers, meant to be shared alongside words murmured gently, as early evening stretched into evening, evening into night.

Ndongo Passy, Grekpoubou and the children had all eaten. No one was thinking of sleep as they waited for the rain that was gathering in the clouds in preparation for nightfall. They were simply waiting. Lidou, who they'd known so intimately, was gone. Each person in their own way was thinking about their own death. Death shakes men and women just as the wind shakes the leaves of the trees. For some, death is a nagging fear that accompanies them every day; for others it's expected but never considered. Others still yearn for the relief of it.

Ndongo Passy and Grekpoubou sat like two lovers under

the mango tree, holding each other tight, dabbing each other's cheeks where the tears had streaked them. The hearts inside their chests beat to the same rhythm. They'd loved the same man, each in her own way. It hadn't always been easy – you can't be a co-wife without a few scowls and sighs – but that night, Lidou's death had brought them close, made them twins, women even more like sisters than sisters were. The two oil lamps at the entrance to the compound cast the softest light possible, as if they knew discretion was required: less light might mean less suffering.

Around midnight, an advance guard of fat raindrops began to splatter here and there. The neighbours who'd stayed brought their mats closer to the trunk of the mango tree for shelter. The children and Yaché were asleep by now in the living room. When the rain became heavy, no longer playful but enraged, people started to withdraw one by one to the living room, until it was packed like a tin of sardines. Someone started to sing:

> *Mawa a gbou bè ti mbi*
> *Mawa a gbou bè ti mbi*
> *Mawa a gbou bè ti mbi*
> *Chéri a zia na congé ohooo*
> *Mawa gbou bè ti mbi ohooo*
> *Mawa...*
> *Mawa...*
> *Mawa...*
> *Tè kobè gui mbi oko ohooo*
> *Sala n'gui a gui mbi oko ohooo*
> *Lango na da gui mbi oko ohooo*
> *Mawa...*

45

Mawa...
Mawa...
Na péko ti lo ohooo
Gui gui mbi oko ohooo
Mawa a gbou bè ti mbi ohoo

Softly, solemnly, everyone else took up the chorus. The rain continued, the wind rose, thunder rumbled. The poor sky was slashed from side to side by the machete strokes of lightning. Despite their anxiety, the people in the living room kept singing, their voices and their hearts in tune. It was then that Ndongo Passy stood up and helped Grekpoubou up too. The two widows went outside into the rain. The others watched them go as if this was natural. The widows had barely crossed the threshold when a flash of lightning brighter than all the others lit them up for a long moment, turning the two women, already soaked, into stars of the night. They disappeared.

Ndongo Passy led Grekpoubou to the outdoor kitchen at the side of the compound. The pans were clattering in the rain and wind. Ndongo Passy picked up the axe they used to chop wood for the fire.

'What, my sister?' Grekpoubou asked.

'Follow me,' said Ndongo Passy. 'You need to live, and I do too.'

Grekpoubou followed her into the night, to the closed door of her own room. With the precision of a woodcutter in the forest, Ndongo Passy broke the door down with repeated blows from the axe. Her arms were strong: it was done in no time.

'Go on, sister, take all your things out of that room. They

46

belong to you. Don't forget anything, or that hawk Zouaboua will steal it from you. I'm going to do the same in my own room.'

The others continued to sing, perhaps a little louder than before, perhaps to drown out the sounds of the axe. Ndongo Passy broke open the door of her own room just as quickly. She put a clean sheet on top of the bed and threw everything she could find into it. She filled three sheets in this way. Money, photos, documents and anything else valuable went into a bag.

She went back to find Grekpoubou, to make sure she was claiming everything that was hers.

'Sister, don't forget your Singer!'

She grabbed the sewing machine herself and put it into a blue bag that had once held fifty kilos of Thai rice. She moved towards Lidou's office, axe in hand. Some people might have called her crazy at that moment, a witch; others might have called her a warrior. Either way, if Zouaboua had presented himself right then, she would've chopped his limbs into a thousand pieces and cooked them. That night, Ndongo Passy was no longer a saint or a mother: she was an injured, ferocious beast.

It took one strike of the axe to break the lock off the door to Lidou's office. The door swung open gently, as if pushed by an invisible hand. Ndongo Passy turned on the light. She behaved as if she was implementing orders, a plan she'd been learning by heart for weeks. She smashed Lidou's laptop: she knew computers had hiding places for secrets, and she didn't want Zouaboua getting his hands on whatever they were; let Lidou take them to his grave. She opened the drawers, striking them with the axe if they were locked, and found bank papers, insurance papers, property and accountancy papers. She found two envelopes, one containing eight hundred thousand francs, the other two million. Lidou was wise; he'd never put all of his money in the bank. Everyone in the town knew that tomorrow, or in a month, or before Mother's Day came around again, there could be another rebellion, with death and pillaging and ridiculous military people setting fire to buildings, banks included. When that happened, your money was lost, and you had to keep quiet about having had it in the first place.

Ndongo Passy found two cheque books. She'd never signed a cheque in her life, but she knew what they were used for.

The raid completed, Ndongo Passy sent Grekpoubou, along with the half-asleep Gbandagba, to take her booty to her parents' house. 'When you've done that,' she said, 'Come back and get the rest of what's yours. Leave it all with your parents.'

Grekpoubou and Gbandagba left in a very yellow taxi, washed clean by the rain, to make their first delivery of the night.

The next morning, night gently passed the baton on to day and life continued. One man was dead. Somewhere else, another man felt alive again; somewhere a person felt sorrow, another person felt joy; one woman awoke not yet aware she'd conceived a child with her lover the night before; another awoke not yet aware she'd been infected with the sickness by her lover the night before; in towns and in the bush, brand new widows were about to be robbed by the families of the deceased. Sometimes, the sacred unit of the family has cruelty

48

and deceit at its heart.

Ndongo Passy slept. When she awoke, she understood that her life was about to change completely. She felt a vibration at her chest: she'd taken Lidou's telephone. The message said, 'Celebrate St Valentine's Day with Orange! Spend 2500 francs per week to enter a free draw to win a dream beach holiday for two.'

She smiled to herself and thought, 'A beach holiday for two, for Grekpoubou and me, why not?'

5

In PK 10, Poto-Poto neighbourhood, they were about to strike the *linga* drum to announce Lidou's death. A wake was a grand occasion: people were already gathering, eager for the opportunity to let their tears flow in company. The tom-tom player began to beat out his rhythms. It was as if a termite mound was emptying, as a whole silent population assembled in the compound.

They say that a truce should hold until the dead person is in the ground. Zouaboua didn't care for that convention; he was already weighing up his options. He'd grown up with Lidou; they'd been like friends and brothers. If an inheritance could fill Zouaboua's pockets, at least something good would've come from Lidou's death. Zouaboua had already made good progress in that direction: he wasn't going to let a couple of gossiping wives stand in his way.

'Are you all right, Zouaboua?'

'I'm fine, Songowali.'

'Where are your reading glasses?'

'They're here.'

He took the glasses from his shirt pocket. Their magnifying lenses allowed him to decipher even the tiniest words on the box of *La Vache qui rit*, his preferred soft, creamy cheese. On the wall above his head, the clock tick-tocked, reminding the living that time marched on.

Songowali pulled up a chair in front of her cousin. She wore a long-sleeved outfit. She passed Zouaboua a two-sided sheet, fresh from the printers: the funeral programme.

'I think it's good, but tell me what you think. Check every word.'

Zouaboua's spectacles gave him a serious air. A professional face reader would've said butter wouldn't melt in his mouth.

On the front of the funeral programme, the name of the deceased appeared above a framed colour portrait. It was an ordinary portrait, an old one Songowali had got from their mother. It gave no clue as to whether the person in question was a villain or a saint. The text beneath the portrait read: *Born 12th December 1962, Obo, deceased 5th February 2011, Bangui.*

The other side of the sheet had the order of ceremony followed by a biographical note. Through his serious lenses, Zouaboua checked both paragraphs for errors. He read aloud:

8th February 2011

Public vigil at the family home, PK 10

9th February 2011

7.30-8.30: Collection of the body, Bangui Community Hospital
8.30-9.00: Laying out of the body at the family home, PK 10 (opposite the ALIMA building)
9.00-10.30: Entertainment and devotional chanting
10.30-11.00: Sermon
11.00-12.00: Speeches by relatives
12.00-12.30: Placing of wreaths
12.30-13.00: Departure for the family tomb, Ngounaja village (PK 13, Damara road)

– Internment
– Return to Bangui
– Light refreshments. End of ceremony.

He said, 'This is an excellent programme, Songowali! You write well; it's obvious you were chewing your pencil at school right up to the fifth year!'

Songowali smiled. She watched Zouaboua as he read on in silence, his lips moving a little, as if he was just learning to read. His face took on a melancholy expression (everyone experiences joy and pain: even a rebel, after years spent killing for fun, might suddenly crumple at the sight of a small gazelle downed by a stray round from his Kalashnikov).

Zouaboua deciphered the text, syllable by syllable, word by word:

Faustin Lidou

Born 12th December 1962, Ligoua, Obo
child of Magberessié Léon (dec.)
and Noguigoro Bernadette

– Primary school in Obo (Haut-M'bomou Préfecture)

– Apprenticeship in masonry, Banganssou

– Founder of Lidou Construction Ltd (building and public works company, all categories), 1998.

He leaves two wives and five children, as well as a truck, a car and various other goods.

He also leaves his plate of yabanda and his glass of kangoya, which he enjoyed every day.

'Congratulations, Songowali, it's really very good. If you're still around when my turn comes, I want you writing my funeral programme. Go and get three hundred copies printed straightaway, nicely cut and folded. I'll wait here.'

The compound was already packed with people. The white plastic hired chairs had been set out. Two pots of food sat on their hearth stones, ready to be licked by the flames, to provide sustenance to the guests who'd already arrived and those still to come.

Lidou and Songowali's mother, born in nineteen some-thing or other, looked in the region of eighty. Their father, no longer in the land of the living, was both absent and excused. The family was large and ever-expanding; this was a chance for its members to discover new cousins, great-great or second or once-removed whatevers; people who might or might not feel like family. Like all recently-deceased persons, Lidou would've been astonished to witness so many friends and relatives gathered in one place: a dead man has far more of both than a living man.

Zouaboua wanted a nice photo to immortalise the wake. His little digital camera had recently been stolen, so he had to make do with his phone. This was already great theatre, and they were only at Act I. He already had Acts II, III and IV planned out in his head, and was confident he could pen an Act V as grand and beautiful as those of the white men's tragedies he'd seen in his youth, during the time of Dacko II's presidency. Those plays had broadened his horizons; it was watching them over and over again that had made him the cultured soul he was today. He intercepted Songowali, on her way back from the printers, and declaimed, 'For whom are these snakes that hiss around your heads?'

'What did you say, Zouaboua?'

He came close, and with all the seriousness of the dignitaries from the Church of the Prophetic Christ who'd recently turned up in Bangui, he repeated Racine's immortal line (slightly confusing its words this time) in Songowali's ear like a mysterious code: 'For whom are these snakes that hiss around our heads?'

Songowali stared at him. 'Are you some Pygmy from the forest, talking about snakes like that?'

'The pygmies have no fear of snakes. I do though.'

Zouaboua went to his room and poured a double measure of *Bamara a lango* into a large glass. He needed to re-heat his blood before going to face the widows. He climbed into his pick-up. The motor purred softly, as if unwilling to disturb the chanting coming from the crowded compound. Religious chants were easy, Zouaboua thought, especially alongside other people and when you'd known the words your entire life. Religion was like politics: there was no point paying attention to the content. Everyone knew a Gbaya was always right in Gbaya country, a Banda in a Banda region, and the Pope had the last word in the Vatican.

Songowali was quiet as they drove. She'd come along because of course she wanted her piece of the inheritance pie, maybe a little bit more than her piece. Of course she wanted to guzzle as much of that pie as she could. What a fine word, guzzle, come from Europe to Africa and spreading itself through Bangui. From the minister of something or other to the illiterate inhabitant of the smallest village or the most isolated scrap of forest, whether they knew the word or not, everyone felt the compulsion to guzzle as much as they could whenever they got the chance. Still, Songowali was quiet. Zouaboua's behaviour was alarming her just a little. Her cousin was a man who overstepped the mark many times a day. His latest plan it seemed, involved holding up people's lives the way a highwayman holds up cars. Songowali had thrown in her lot with him, though; if you loved the dog you had to love its fleas.

Zouaboua decided against parking in the courtyard of his deceased cousin's compound. His two enemies were capable of anything, including taking their fingernails to his pick-up. He parked at the foot of the last set of steps in the Cité Christophe. The car would be fine there: some French policemen had even made the neighbourhood their home.

Zouaboua was dressed simply, in a bright, traditional *pagne*. Songowali, in black trousers and an orange top, resembled a rep for a phone company, or for the president's political party perhaps.

Zouaboua quickly assessed the scene in the courtyard. The co-widows, their five children and a dozen neighbours were all there, still grieving for Lidou. Zouaboua strode towards the group like a general crossing a battlefield. Songowali followed close behind, his shadow.

Ndongo Passy didn't even glance at Zouaboua. She knew he was a man with fingers as sticky as a tree frog's; she didn't want to cause unnecessary strain to her eye muscles by looking at him. She smiled, with her lips and with her heart. With her head, she gave the tiniest nod towards her co-widow, who sat as still as a fallen tree.

Four or five seconds passed, then a roar like that of a lion with a thorn in its nose echoed around the courtyard. Ndongo Passy had to use great restraint not to turn her head and smile. She'd been waiting to hear a roar of pain coming from that jumped-up showman, and it was pleasing to her ears. Zouaboua appeared in front of her, bellowing, 'Thief! Thief!'

'What's the problem, Zouaboua?'

'You broke the doors down, you stole from me! You're a thief! You and your co-widow will pay for this!'

'Pay?' Ndongo Passy burst out laughing. It wasn't the old laugh that had flown from her lips at least ten times a day until now, but a new, a vengeful, taunting laugh, a laugh that needled at Zouaboua's heart, that branded him pitiful, someone who stole from widows. If it had been a man mocking him in this way, Zouaboua might've contented himself with some choice insults, but this was a woman, two women, harassing him with laughter and smiles. It was intolerable. He leapt at Ndongo Passy, foaming at the mouth, fists clenched, ready to beat her to a pulp.

Ndongo Passy was ready. When Zouaboua leapt, she stepped aside. He landed half on top of her, half in the dust. Grekpoubou stood up. Songowali reached out to grab her round the middle, but Grekpoubou was also prepared. The two women rolled to the ground, their bodies fused together like the two halves of a kola nut, their limbs intertwined like a needle and its thread. They beat at each other with their heads and their feet, small cries of 'Oh! Oh!' coming from one or other or both of them.

The neighbours and children formed a loose circle around the four fighters. Ndongo Passy boiled with the force of her rage; an electric energy buzzed through her limbs. She darted away from Zouaboua, so he couldn't land a single punch, and lashed out instinctively with her elbows and her knees, devising her own new variety of martial art. Zouaboua lost a tooth and began to bleed from his mouth. He made the mistake of moving his hand towards the place, breaking his concentration. Ndongo Passy launched a furious strike, jamming her knee between his legs. He cried, 'Aieeeeeaieeeeeaieeeee!' A new round commenced.

Grekpoubou and Songowali found themselves separated, standing beside each other. Ndongo Passy clapped as Zouaboua searched in his trousers with both hands for his two lost kola nuts.

The co-widows' victory was short-lived. Someone had called the police, and they arrived quickly for once. Who had done this and why was unclear – this was no public order disturbance, but a private fight in a private compound – but two dilapidated yellow taxis, practically wrecks, pulled up and spewed out seven policemen. The sergeant, a vicious bulldog type, recognised Zouaboua immediately. He went over to help him to his feet. The crowd watched in silence as the police organised themselves into their customary threatening poses, truncheons and MAS 36 rifles poised.

Zouaboua was the same height as the sergeant; it was easy for him to whisper a few words into the man's ear while he got his breath back and established, via a tweak that produced a slightly less violent pain than the one they'd suffered just before, that his kola nuts were still attached.

The sergeant responded with a sort of belch, roughened to a growl by twenty years of smoking. His men immediately captured the co-widows, squeezing their prisoners close for a furtive feel of their bodies before flinging them into the taxis.

A few minutes later, head down, testicles still on fire, Zouaboua was back at the wheel of his own car. Songowali sat beside him, looking as bedraggled as a cloth that had been used to do the cleaning for the entire dry season.

'The death penalty, that's what those bitches deserve!' shouted Zouaboua. Songowali made no reply. As they drew up near the police station and Dr Chouaib's clinic next door to it, Zouaboua continued, 'They'll pay for this! If the police don't kill them, I'll do it myself, to avenge my cousin. To do that to me! To resist me, to attack me! Me! Don't they know that I'm somebody?!'

At that moment, if he'd been a reasonable person as well as a somebody, he would've popped into Dr Chouaib's clinic to get his intimate anatomy checked over. He might also have considered the old saying that no canoe is too big to capsize.

6

The two taxis had only just turned the corner by the petrol station on to the main avenue when a couple of the neighbours who'd witnessed the events, Sendagbia and Kangalé, put their heads together and agreed the neighbourhood chief should be notified. Hopefully, if they explained what had happened, he would help them rescue Ndongo Passy and Grekpoubou from the police. Kangalé, who was chronically unemployed, said to Sendagbia, 'Do you have credit, sister?'

Sendagbia checked her phone. '800 francs. That's enough.'

Like everyone, they knew the number of the chief, Kpokolo, by heart. He was probably still at the Social Affairs office in the town hall. He was always the last to leave. He answered after two rings.

'Hello chief, it's your sister Sendagbia.'

'What is it?'

'You need to come to Lidou's place right away. Shameful things have been happening here.'

'What is it? Tell me!'

'Lidou's cousin Zouaboua's been fighting with the wives of our deceased. Ndongo Passy beat him. It's not good, not good at all. Come!'

'I'll be there immediately, or near enough.'

'Immediately, not near enough!'

'I'm coming.'

Kpokolo was young and seemed even younger. He took his job in social affairs and his status in the neighbourhood seriously. He grabbed his helmet and climbed on to his bike. When it came to avoiding Bangui potholes, a motorbike beat a Mercedes, black or white, hands down. As promised, Kpokolo arrived quickly. Sendagbia and Kangalé already had matters in hand: they'd gone down the streets shouting: those who'd heard that call were now passing it on to others. The whole neighbourhood was being summoned to Lidou's compound. There was so much commotion Kpokolo had wondered if there was some sort of election meeting going on.

'The police abducted those women!'

'Which women?'

'Ndongo Passy and Grekpoubou!'

'Ah.'

The chief had known Ndongo Passy for years. He'd often joked with her, 'If I hit a tree on my bike and write myself off, you'd make a great neighbourhood chief.' It was true that Ndongo Passy already dealt ably with a great number of local problems.

But Kpokolo wasn't the current neighbourhood chief for

nothing. He sat down on the steps to the living room and had everything explained to him twice, by two different people. He knew the person who shouts loudest isn't always the one who's right, and he knew that to prise the two women out of the grubby hands of the police he'd need to have the right words in his mouth about the whys and the wherefores. When he stood up, he announced, to the delight of those who were itching to set off, 'Let's go to the police station. They're our women. Follow me. No shouting!'

It was less than fifteen minutes' walk to the police station, and the eagerness of the group meant they got there in ten. Kpokolo had phoned ahead, so the police superintendent was expecting them. When they arrived, they found Ndongo Passy and Grekpoubou behind bars. No one had yet had the time or the inclination to question them. The police were busy beating up a young boy who'd stolen two mobile phones and had the misfortune to be caught in the act by the owner of the second. The neighbours waited in the foyer, treated to the desperate cries of the young man and the laughter of the police.

Zouaboua and Songowali, their composure recovered, were waiting there too, to make their statement accusing the two widows of breaking and entering, poisoning, sorcery, terrorism, and a lack of respect for persons of importance such as Zouabaoua.

When the small crowd arrived behind its leader, Zouaboua recognised Georgine and Mbilakoué and understood the situation. He dragged Songowali out to the pick-up. As he started the ignition he said, 'This is heating up, we'd better make ourselves scarce; that crazy crowd could roast us alive.'

The punishing heat had finished with Bangui for the day.

The light was beginning to fade. The police station of the first arrondissement wasn't far from the presidential palace. The superintendent knew that to let a crowd mill around the area like an ants nest wasn't a good idea, especially at election time. He came out to talk to the chief.

The chief was as cunning as a *makako*. He began by flattering the superintendent a little, then he said he knew from experience the best way to calm the women of his neighbourhood down. Finally he swore on an imaginary Bible and an imaginary Qu'ran that he would personally return the two widows to the station to give their account of events if required.

His breath was not wasted. The superintendent released the women. The crowd applauded them as if they'd just been elected deputies, and gathered round to escort them back home. At the compound, Grekpoubou's two eldest daughters, Ibenga and Mazenga, had helped Yaché to make food for themselves, their younger sister Tangani and their brothers Gbandagba and Koutia. Now they were all digging into a plate of manioc leaves and plantain, along with an onion and tomato omelette that Ndongo Passy and Grekpoubou had left for them, each clutching their piece firmly in a portion of bread.

The co-widows and their children gathered beneath the mango tree, lit up by their two oil lamps. Zouaboua was no more cunning than the next *makako*, but he'd spent ten years in government and fifteen in the office of an international insurance broker, so he had connections. He'd asked a friend who worked for the electricity board to cut off the electricity in Lidou's compound.

It was the first time since Lidou's death that the whole

family had been alone together. The children had begun to feel anxious about the future. They now understood that if Zouaboua got his way, they'd have to go and live somewhere else, probably change schools. They didn't like that idea: all of them wanted to remain in their father's house, to keep their school and neighbourhood friends. Even the youngest among them had grasped that their mothers were suffering pain and worry that was perhaps even greater than their own. Gbandagba, the oldest, observed, 'No scales can weigh a person's pain. Not even the Lebanese sell such a thing.'

Koutia, just a little younger than his brother, replied, 'You can weigh and measure everything. The circumference of the earth, the distance from here to the moon…'

The girls listened, intrigued. Gbandagba asked, 'What's the use of knowing the distance from here to the moon?'

Koutia had all the answers that evening. He said, 'The use is knowing it. Knowing is what matters.'

'You have a busy brain tonight, Koutia!'

It was true. Perhaps because he was sad and had searched in his soul for the source of his tears, Koutia was philosophising like a professor without even realising it. The girls got up, cleaned the stovetop and the big serving plate, then went to have their showers. The children had understood that it was time to leave their mothers alone.

Mother moon was wandering across the sky as if nothing had changed, with a few thousand daughters following in her wake. Together they cast enough light for the night not to be completely black: shadows dappled the ground like messages. Ndongo Passy and Grekpoubou sat on a mat beneath the mango tree, their backs against the trunk, staring into the night. They held hands. Without them really registering it, their hearts were drawing closer with every breath. It was the first time they'd sat together like this, entirely united. The force binding them was unhappiness. Softly, they began to speak. Ndongo Passy went first, addressing herself partly to the mangoes, partly to Grekpoubou, partly to the night: 'When I was a girl in the village, I thought I'd grow up and never die and have a husband forever. A husband just for me. When Lidou married me at the Bangui town hall, I felt the same: that he and I would never die. But now he's dead. His life is over. And my life…? And your life…?'

As she murmured the last words, Ndongo Passy squeezed the hand of her co-widow a little tighter. There was more than a minute of silence in the courtyard. Somewhere in the neighbourhood, an orchestra was playing to celebrate the election result. Grekpoubou said, 'You know sister, that I never loved Lidou with all my heart. I loved him so I could come and live in town. When he asked my parents for me, I had my eye on a boy in the village, a boy who used to go hunting with a bow and arrow. But even before the dowry, Lidou had handed over five goats! Five! When I came to Bangui, I didn't even know he already had a wife. It didn't make any difference to me, though.'

'I know that, Grekpoubou. I understood that, but I didn't want you here. I turned my back on Lidou for a long time because of it. After a while, I let him love me again the way he wanted to, but I never made gestures of love myself. And now you and I have found each other.'

'What do you mean?'

'I mean that you're here and I'm here. I've come to

understand that life is never afterwards, never tomorrow. It's only now.'

After a little while she continued, still holding her sister's hand. 'Suddenly we're both sad, both being abused by Zouaboua and the other one, Songowali. But tomorrow will be here soon. We have to keep on living, for ourselves and for our children.'

'Yes. Our children.'

'My womb only made one child. One is only one. It's not enough, and now all of that's over for me.'

'You should go to a healer, talk to him about your womb!'

'Does an honest woman talk to a man about her womb?'

'A healer's not like a real man!'

'Hmm… but now Lidou's not here any more, and I've got old.'

'No!'

'What do you mean no?'

'You're a young, beautiful woman! You're my big sister, but you're more beautiful than me. And everyone in the neighbourhood listens to you, even the chief. You went to school!'

'Not enough, only a little bit.'

They fell silent, but remained sitting, hand in hand. Perhaps they were listening to the great voice of time echoing in their ears.

When they got up, the mango tree was still in its usual place in the courtyard, the sky still hung up above, as proud as ever. The two women though were perhaps not exactly the same. It is possible to be reborn, or at least to make a shift, within one life. Ndongo Passy and Grekpoubou didn't know it, but the next day they would be almost completely new. As soon as they spoke new words to describe themselves, conjured up new pictures to draw themselves, their mirrors would show them to be transformed.

They took their shower together, splashing around in the dark. Then they lay down on a mat in the living room. Without discussing it, they'd agreed not to sleep alone in their separate rooms. They closed their eyes in peace, without fearing bad dreams.

7

A single hand can't clap. The opposition candidates all knew that. Perhaps it was this reality that caused them to withdraw from the competition, leaving the field clear for the outgoing president. When he was incoming again, they left him alone to try to applaud himself. When the results came in, the outgoing president had not won the first round with 120% of the vote. He could have, if he'd wanted, but he'd chosen 66%. That was hardly greedy, but as everyone knows, the opposition is never satisfied. The four unsuccessful candidates had already had their chance to guzzle all they could of the country's riches, but they wanted to carry on guzzling, to gorge themselves until they burst, like frogs trying to grow as big as cows. One former president, now turned opposition candidate, was making a brazen attempt to have his manioc and eat it. The former rebel candidate, the former prime minister candidate and the former deputy candidate were all cut from the same cloth. Points one, two, three, 100 and 1000 of all of their manifestos were their own guzzling. Guzzling was the most refined expression of the electoral practice of the republic. A more accurate electoral jingle than those actually in use that year might have been, 'Give me your vote and I'll guzzle your *gozo*, your gold and your goat!'

The life of the republic would continue to be marked by interminable electoral debate until the second round, to elect the new deputies, and the inauguration of the re-elected president on March 15th. When that day came, Ndongo Passy and Grekpoubou would be a little more widowed. After that day, and for the entire length of the presidential mandate, they would become more and more widowed, or perhaps less and less. No one could predict what the future held for them: perhaps their lives would slip through their fingers like wet soap, or perhaps, as Ndongo Passy preferred to believe, their days, informed by their suffering, would begin to be painted in the *biani biani* blue that never fades, the blue of a dry season sky.

As the united and intractable opposition candidates expressed their outrage on *Radio Ndéké Luka*, Ndongo Passy and Grekpoubou were making themselves beautiful to say their final goodbyes to Lidou, whose open coffin would be installed in PK 10 at midday. They knew this because Songowali had dropped one of her freshly-printed funeral programmes as she fled from their compound. The co-widows stood together in the living room, tying on floor-length black *pagnes* sewn in rich bazin fabric. Their hair was tucked into black silk headscarves. With their black skin and black clothes, they looked every inch new widows, perhaps the most beautiful black widows in town. Their sons Gbandagba and Koutia were dressed for the occasion too, in black jeans and black T-shirts.

'Don't be scared, sister. He's our husband. No one can stop us crying over his coffin.'

'They can start another fight.'

'Hmm.'

The co-widows and their sons took a taxi to PK 10, Poto-Poto neighbourhood. As they approached the compound, set back from the road, Grekpoubou dropped back behind Ndongo Passy.

They could hear a band playing and several dozen voices singing a sort of religious rock. Ndongo Passy turned and said, 'Walk beside me, Grekpoubou. We were his co-wives!'

In the compound, a large number of women and a few men sat in the shade; on the ground, on chairs and on benches. They barely glanced at the widows and their sons as they made their way around the side of the house. A tantalising smell of manioc leaves and taro tickled their nostrils. They found the coffin; right beside it, almost body to body with Lidou where he lay between his wooden planks and his glass, were his mother, his sister Songowali and some of his cousins. Other people sat nearby in white plastic chairs; the non-relatives, the non-invited and all the random workers who'd built Lidou's villas for him.

Ndongo Passy walked straight ahead, holding Grekpoubou by the hand. The two children followed. None of them saw the stirring in the midst of the rows of chairs that held at least a hundred waiting people. Suddenly two dozen arms, legs and eyes were moving in their direction. The band continued to play, the bass of the drums seeming to dictate the movements of the crowd. The attacking arms seized the co-widows from the side and pulled them to the ground. Voices joined together in shouts. Lidou remained immobile.

There was no fight. The widows and their sons were powerless against Zouaboua's army. The crowd beat them up as if they were in an American film on TV; it was a battle to music with baddies who didn't know when to stop.

Grekpoubou had a bleeding cheek, one eye swollen shut. Ndongo Passy's *pagne* was ripped and her headscarf had disappeared. The two boys were crying. Four hands appeared, along with some soothing words for the losing team. The mothers and boys were dragged to a truck and deposited on the passenger bench at the back. It was Lidou's truck, their rescuers a builder, who was driving, and an accountant who'd worked for *Lidou Construction Ltd (building and public works company, all categories)*.

As the injured widows were being driven back home, Zouaboua was stepping up to the mike to read Lidou's elegy. It was composed of hollow phrases composed of hollow words. The audience had heard the same words countless times at other funeral services. The dead person was always wonderful. No one ever said, 'The deceased was a bastard.' The day the elected president died, the day his united and intransigent opponents died, people would hold forth about what responsible spouses, brothers, friends and citizens they were, how perfectly they'd balanced the sharp with the sweet, how virtuously they appreciated both the nationalist *gozo* and the republican plantain.

If the dead had all been as perfect as their funeral elegies suggested, life in the republic would've been a beautiful thing.

Such are the conventions of life and of death.

'That Zouaboua is a swine.'

That phrase had become the toothpick in every mouth around the widows' neighbourhood. The day after Lidou's burial, Ndongo Passy and Grekpoubou were starting to recover from the punches and slaps they'd received. They were a little disoriented. They both knew they had to take their lives into their own hands. A friend passed by, selling traditional Cameroonian robes designed for International Women's Day on March 8th. Ndongo Passy bought two; red for herself, green for her co-widow. 'We're women,' she said, 'So this is for us. Look, a nice design of a woman on top of a lovely round earth.'

Grekpoubou, who could read very little French, tried to decipher the letters below the image of the woman and the planet earth: *International Women's Day*. 'Those words are in English, like they speak in Nigeria and Tanzania,' Ndongo Passy explained.

Grekpoubou's daughters had done the washing and bundled it into two buckets. Yaché, who'd been doing all the housework for weeks, had now left to return to her village. The two brothers, Gbandagba and Koutia, were busy making themselves new catapults.

When Zouaboua's pick-up drew into the courtyard, the co-widows weren't surprised. They were alone, in a no-man's land between one life and the next. They were vulnerable and tired. The pick-up was full; not quite as full as a bush-taxi heading for Mbaïki or Damara, but almost. Eight people spewed out of the double cabin, half a dozen jumped down from the bed at the back.

Zouaboua placed himself in front of the women, his disordered army massed behind him. He shouted, 'Leave! In fifteen minutes, my cousin Lidou's compound will belong to me and to the rest of his family. You have fifteen minutes to get out.'

The vicious words that came from his lips seemed to amuse him greatly. His henchmen sneered nastily in support. They were armed with truncheons; two had machetes. How much had Zouaboua paid them? A thousand francs? Just five hundred?

Ndongo Passy didn't waste her breath responding. To her co-widow she said softly, 'Grekpoubou, we have to go. Fill a couple of bags with your things and the children's things. I'll do the same.' Even more quietly, perhaps only to herself, she added, 'We've already taken all the important stuff.'

They were ready in no time. It was the smallest house move imaginable. Each widow had two bags. The girls had their school satchels on their backs and the buckets of wet washing in their hands. The boys just had their satchels.

They left Lidou's compound in silence. As soon as they'd stepped out of the gate, Ndongo Passy handed an envelope to Grekpoubou. She'd been keeping it underneath her *pagne* ever since the night they'd broken the doors down and taken their essential belongings away.

'Take that, sister. It's your share, for today. There's a small fortune in there for you and your children: five hundred thousand francs. It was in Lidou's office. Zouaboua can cry and scream as much as he likes; I've got the money that was in the drawer and that bastard will never get the chance to spend it. You know everything we said, you know how to contact me, I know how to contact you. We'll fight this. We'll go to court. While we're waiting for that, you'll be OK with your parents in Ouango, I'll be OK with my old folks back in PK 26.'

The co-widows squeezed each other tight. The children had already stopped two taxis. Grekpoubou left quickly in the first, Ndongo Passy settled herself in the other. Just as her son leapt up beside her, she heard a scream. Zouaboua fell down like a demon attacked. The taxi started up.

'What happened?'

Gbandagba didn't reply. 'What was it?' insisted Ndongo Passy.

He showed her his catapult. He'd used his good aim to take his own small revenge.

It's difficult for tired parents to see their child return with children. When Grekpoubou came back to her parents' house, they felt out of their depth. They'd learned day by day of Zouaboua's actions towards the widows: they understood the situation without needing to exchange a word. They settled their daughter and their grandchildren in their home. To reassure them, Grekpoubou gave them a hundred thousand francs straightaway, enough for everyone to eat for several days, even weeks.

When Ndongo Passy arrived with her son at her childhood home, there was nothing of the beggar or the defeated about her. Her widowhood, her fate, her bruised life, all had only made her stronger and more beautiful. Before arriving, she'd bought three chickens, a basin of manioc and a banana republic of plantain. She put all of this down beside her bags in the courtyard. After briefly describing the most recent events and the details of her new situation to her parents, her uncle, two cousins and the various children who lived there, she added, 'It's OK. My life's been tied in a knot that I can't undo with my fingers, but I'll use my teeth.'

A mat was unrolled for her inside and she lay down. By the time she dropped off into a restoring sleep, the three chickens had been killed and the *gozo* was being prepared.

8

Kwa na Kwa was the slogan of the outgoing and incoming
president's party, KNK its name. It sounded beautiful in
Sango, the national language and the beating lexical heart
of the republic, and it meant '*work, only work*'. Throw in an
impartial justice system and your entire population is on an
equal footing. Grand and impressive concepts. Except that feet
in the republic were far from equal: some were bare; some were
clad in flimsy flip flops; some sported Chinese Converses, or
Converses re-christened Adidas or Nike; and still others got
their kicks in patent leather pumps.

Kwa na Kwa would provide for every man and woman.
Except that men and women couldn't decide any better than
God could what was just. When even God sometimes messed
things up, what could possibly be expected from people?

These were the thoughts that swarmed inside Ndongo

Passy's head during those days and nights. They were there when she was with her child, they were there when she was talking to her parents and her cousins. They were there when she stood naked under the shower and felt the weight of her breasts, soft as manioc or coffee powder.

It was no good dreaming of justice; it was just like with the elections. Ndongo Passy had come to understand something that all the somebodies who'd chewed their pencils until the very last day of the last year of university pretended not to understand: there was no justice. She knew this, but still she wanted to try. She was like the good citizen who goes back to vote again and again, hoping every time that a miracle will occur. She had a little money; she could afford to take her case before the judge. She'd been thinking about it since Zouaboua's first attack, she'd discussed it with her co-widow. Her mind was made up. She would prepare her notes and the Sango would creep out of her mouth and into the ears of the judge until he knew the whole of her story. It was out of necessity that the *makako* climbed the tree. Ndongo Passy would climb, in search of justice for herself, her co-widow and their children. Why shouldn't she?

'Hello, Jean de Dieu?'

'What can I do for you, Ndongo Passy?'

'I need a good lawyer to plead my case. You know, I think…'

'I know.'

'I thought you might have come across one; more than one, perhaps…'

'I have. I'm on my way.'

'Be quick. I'll give you the taxi money when you get here.'

Jean de Dieu was the child of Ndongo Passy's mother's brother. Soon he would don the lawyer's robe himself; for now he was still in training.

It was a Saturday morning. Ndongo Passy sat at the door of her family's compound, selling white flour and firewood, just as she'd done at the door of Lidou's compound. A small radio beside her played a tune by *Sapéké Musica*. After that a programme called '*Open Heart*' began. Ndongo Passy listened distractedly to an inhabitant of PK 5 intersection praising his preferred candidate in the deputies' election. This man, someone close to power, exaggerated so much that the more he tried to colour and flavour his words, the duller and blander they became, until they no longer even sounded like words at all.

Jean de Dieu arrived, looking serious. He greeted his relative. She led him into the courtyard and they sat on stools opposite each other in the shade of a twisted acacia tree. Gbandagba brought them some water before taking his mother's place outside the house to sell the manioc and wood.

Jean de Dieu already knew the co-widows' story, but he listened all the same. When Ndongo Passy had finished speaking, he rested his elbows on his knees, interlaced his fingers, and as serious as a doctor about to deliver a dire diagnosis, he declared, 'All right, Ndongo Passy. It's going to be OK. A good lawyer will help you and your co-widow and your children get your inheritance back.'

His face lit up as he added, 'I know just the person.'

'Which person is that?'

'A person who only started practising last year, but knows what it takes to win and likes helping women.'

'Helping women? Why?'

'Because she's a woman herself.'

'Really?'

'Yes. Her father owns the biggest legal firm in Bangui, the one that defends all the whites who work for the big companies. But she's opened her own office.'

'Why would she do that? Why wouldn't she work for her father?'

'Perhaps she didn't want to lick white arses all day long. Anyway, she'll know how to defend you. I have her number. Shall I call her?'

'Yes!'

Jean de Dieu made the call and a secretary arranged a meeting.

Ndongo Passy had asked Grekpoubou to make herself beautiful and be in front of the Cathedral of the Immaculate Conception at 10 am. She'd specified, 'Ten, not half past.' They embraced when they saw each other, and a few happy tears slid from their eyes. Ndongo Passy explained everything to Grekpoubou. She concluded by saying, 'There's no need to be afraid of her; she's a woman like us, and a lawyer who's going to defend us. I'll speak for you, sister.'

Jean de Dieu, waiting by the Saint Theresa school, saw them approaching from a distance. They went together to Catherine Maïgaro's office, which was inside her villa, on the hill. She obviously had no fear of the night goblins people said made their home up there. The lawyer's secretary, who was all smiles and looked like Michelle Obama's twin sister, met them immediately and showed them into a large office. The co-widows were surprised to see that Catherine Maïgaro was a small, delicate-looking person. But as soon as she opened her mouth to say in French, 'Take a seat there opposite me,' her whole demeanour changed. It was a voice that was at once soft and firm.

Jean de Dieu, who knew Catherine well, sat a little further back. Catherine placed her palms flat on the desk. She looked from one widow to the other and said, 'So what's the problem?'

Ndongo Passy had practised what she wanted to say to the lawyer at least a hundred times in her head. Now she was sitting in front of her, she forgot it all. Unusually, she found herself speechless. There was a silence, then Catherine burst out laughing. She'd realised the two women were intimidated by her. She said, 'We have time. I know you know how to speak. We can forget French and speak Sango if you like. The French language is beautiful, but so is our Sango.'

Perhaps it was these words or perhaps it was the smile that came with them that allowed Ndongo Passy to open her mouth. She didn't search her head for the prepared speech; she simply spoke of their lives up until Lidou's death, then of their lives since Lidou's death. She finished by saying, 'They want absolutely everything. They're bad people. What we want is just to be able to live, to bring up our kids.'

Catherine asked some questions, took some notes, then declared, 'Don't worry. I'll defend you. You're no longer alone. The three of us are in this together, and we're going to win. I'll get started on your case immediately. The Family Code is on your side; it enshrines your rights and those of your children.'

She gave a few more details, made a list of the items she

would need, then stood.

'My secretary here will take care of everything else. She's available to see you whenever you need her.'

Ndongo Passy wanted to embrace Catherine in thanks. Only a woman, she thought, could really understand another woman. The secretary told the co-widows and Jean de Dieu, who was taking notes, 'I'll need photocopies of the marriage certificates and the children's birth certificates. If all goes well, then you, Grekpoubou, should get your official share of the inheritance too, even if Lidou married you illegally. You're the mother of four children who bear Lidou's name. That's enough; the new Family Code says so.'

Ndongo Passy paid the secretary fifty thousand francs for the opening of their file. Seeking justice wasn't cheap.

The co-widows walked together to the North Terminus bus station, where Grekpoubou would take the bus to PK 12, then on to PK 26. Grekpoubou had spoken very little all morning. Now she said, 'I'm coming back into town tomorrow with two of the kids. I'll take three nice chickens to Catherine.'

Ndongo Passy hesitated, then turned away from the yellow taxi that would've taken her to the city centre. Instead she began to walk away from the bus station, in the direction of the petrol station. She'd decided to pay a little visit to some former neighbours. She also wanted to pass by Lidou's compound, her former home, the place where she'd lived happily for so long.

Where she used to sit at the gate selling manioc, a man in a chocolate-coloured uniform now sat on a chair. Beside him was something that looked like a baseball bat. When Ndongo Passy was a few steps away from him, he stood up and made some stretching movements. The back of his shirt bore the acronym *BCAGS*. That was the Central African Office of Security and Surveillance. Zouaboua must be really afraid of her to engage a security service to guard the compound. Ndongo Passy murmured to herself, 'Perhaps he's so scared of me he's been pissing the bed.'

She stayed on the other side of the dirt track and walked past slowly, taking tiny steps. She heard a squealing sound coming from the courtyard. Songowali stood with her back to her, hanging washing on the line. Songowali had nine children, with nine different fathers. Her husbands had always disappeared as soon as the baby was born, before Songowali had even had time to get up and re-tie her *pagne*. Ndongo Passy knew this because she'd been friends with Songowali for a long time. That friendship was over now. First, Songowali had started talking behind Ndongo Passy's back about her failure to give Lidou another child. Then there was the theft of the money from their group savings kitty. It was Songowali who'd stolen it, or 'forgotten' to register it in the books, when she was supposed to be keeping the money for the others. To appease the women, who'd been ready to take their revenge on Songowali with rolling pins or machetes, Ndongo Passy had reimbursed them with her own money. After that, Songowali and Ndongo Passy had barely spoken.

In the courtyard, a man's voice was asking whether the water was hot for his shower. So it was in order to house Songowali, her large tribe of children and her new husband that Lidou's family had behaved so badly. Ndongo Passy felt sad. Not for the loss of her compound – she knew she had to wait for the judgement of the court on that – but for

Songowali, who'd been a good person once. She could have carried on being good, but fate had been cruel to her. Ndongo Passy blamed Zouaboua: if you spent time with a hyena, you ended up eating rotten meat. That was what had happened to Songowali.

When she arrived at Georgine's house, Georgine was preparing food: she'd just finished finely chopping koko leaves. The two women embraced warmly. Georgine passed on the latest news: no one in the neighbourhood was happy with the departure of the co-widows; no one was prepared to lend Songowali salt, or matches, or anything else she might need.

As she returned in a taxi to her family's compound in PK 26, Ndongo Passy thought to herself, 'This country should be run by women; real women, like Catherine Maïgaro or Georgine.' She'd been thinking about this so much over the last few days that she now understood that an important woman or a neighbourhood woman would be perfectly capable of the job. A woman, like a man, held her faith in her heart. If the heart used the mouth to speak grand words, like justice, equality and liberty, that was all for the good. If it was only the mouth that spoke, using the words to deceive, that was no good at all.

Catherine worked quickly: she'd set the judicial wheels in motion before the president of the republic had even been inaugurated.

Lidou's relatives had called a family council, and of course it was Zouaboua who'd been designated Lidou's heir. He was authorised to speak for all of them. The family council had been held at Lidou's former home, in the presence of the co-widows and their children. The clan had taken precautions: the co-widows had the right only to listen. Zouboua had then had the verbal proceedings of the meeting ratified, in a public session, by the court.

Catherine had appealed to the regional court because the family council had not taken the widows into consideration. The case of Ndongo Passy vs. Lidou's heirs, represented by Zouaboua, was also scheduled for a public session. Ndongo Passy had invited all the neighbours to come and witness the spectacle of justice. She hoped their presence would bring her and Grekpoubou luck.

Catherine was already there when the co-widows arrived in the courtroom. It was a large room, and it was very full. The judge, flanked by his associate judges, had already begun making judgements. The co-widows sat down beside Jean de Dieu, who continued to discreetly support and advise them. Catherine came up, smiling and confident. She touched the women's hands and said, 'Here we are! I'm pleased. A good judgement is going to be delivered today. In no time at all, you'll be saved!'

On the same row as the women, on the other side of the aisle, sat a very tall man, clearly a Fulani, because he held a pointed leather hat on his knees. He wasn't wearing a lawyer's robe or a suit and tie, but an embroidered *boubou* sewn in rich bazin, as blue as a pristine sky. In one hand he was counting prayer beads. His bearing was proud. Was this a rebel prince come to demand justice from a king?

Men and women can sometimes seem as beautiful and as present as a saint in a church, simply through the way they carry themselves. This Fulani man was like that – beautiful and present. Ndongo Passy didn't notice him immediately, because she only had eyes for the judge, but when she shifted position on the bench, she caught sight of his pointed hat. When she saw its owner, she touched her hand instinctively to her headscarf. The Fulani, who was observing everything keenly, glanced towards her as well. Their eyes met. Did he find her more beautiful than the most beautiful of his cows?

A few of the day's cases had now been dismissed. Catherine made a sign to the co-widows to approach: their turn had come. They got up from the bench and presented themselves before the court, while Zouaboua took his place with his lawyer nearby. Ndongo Passy and Grekpoubou felt even more intimidated than they had on the day they'd gone to vote.

9

For the judge, it was a day like any other. It tickled him a little
to watch the lawyers pop up in front of him every morning,
always with a mobile phone, or even two, in their hands. He
didn't own one himself. Perhaps the lawyers were all waiting
for important communications from the White House or the
Elysée Palace, or the rebels in the north of the country perhaps.

For Ndongo Passy, Grekpoubou and even Zouaboua,
though he was accustomed to making speeches to the ceiling,
the setting was impressive. The image of Justice on the wall
behind the judge gave solemnity to the occasion. After a
moment though, Ndongo Passy's awe subsided and she began
to wonder why the machete held by Justice was twice as long
as those sold in the markets at PK 0 and PK 5.

The judge spoke first, in such a low mumble that those
assembled had to prick up both their ears to hear what he was

saying. The trial had begun.

The audience included a number of the co-widows' neighbours, as well as the president of the Widows Association of Bangui, who sat beside the presenter of the radio programme 'Our Women'. Strangely, the case also seemed to be of some interest to the Fulani prince, who was now positioned prominently in the second row.

Questions were asked, answers given. Zouaboua's lawyer was a tall, thick-set, powerful man. When he spoke he smiled, delighted with himself, showing all his teeth. He recited for the judge all the reasons why, in his opinion, his client had acted within his rights as an honest man and a good citizen. He concluded, 'If the late Lidou was with us now, there is no doubt that it is to his cousin Zouaboua that he would confer all his worldly goods, perhaps even his wives as well!' He bowed to the judge and turned to Catherine, confident of having already convinced the judge and the entire world of his view.

Catherine gave a small cough and looked deep into the judge's eyes, as if she wanted to probe his soul. The judge shifted just a little in his chair. Catherine began by outlining the law that protected her clients and their children. She was impressive, as confident as if she'd been taking a course in African Law for the tenth time, at a big European or American university.

Ndongo Passy and Grekpoubou were proud of their lawyer, even if the technical arguments she was elaborating went over their heads. By the time Catherine had finished, the mouth of Zouaboua's lawyer had closed and all the teeth of his smile had disappeared.

He spoke again, making a face that implied he was a little sorry for the women, and informed the judge that he wished to make him aware of a document; a piece of evidence he had hoped initially not to have to use. The judge showed some surprise, but not as much as Catherine, whose eyes had grown very large.

Zouaboua's lawyer approached the judge and murmured to him, 'This should settle it.'

The judge read to himself every word of the document written by Émile Ngando, doctor at the community hospital. He frowned, then re-read it aloud. The situation for Catherine and her clients seemed desperate. But Catherine counter-attacked, saying, 'This text you've just read, your Honour, brings no new element to the consideration of the legitimate rights of succession that should be accorded to the widows of the late Lidou and their children. Furthermore, in order for that document to carry any weight, we would need a second medical opinion, even an autopsy. My clients cannot be accused of poisoning without the court having access to the judicial conclusions of an inquiry.'

She took a breath and added, addressing both the judge and the painting of Justice on the wall, 'Stealing the inheritance of these children will be stealing their youth and their chance to grow up into good citizens who can help to build this country.' She took another breath. 'These women, Lidou's two widows, have done nothing wrong. They loved their husband: numerous witnesses can attest to that.'

Throwing a black look at Zouaboua, she added, 'These women have never knotted up the rain to stop it from falling.' She turned back to the judge, and indicating Zouaboua, said,

'It is this man and his family who are lawless and faithless.'

The judge had listened and understood. He announced the date of the deliberation. Eight days later, everyone would know their fate. As is common in these cases, the co-widows were so convinced they were in the right that they were certain the judgement would go in their favour. They left the courtroom with Catherine and exchanged a few words outside in the sun, underneath a large poster from the National Anti-Corruption Committee, read, like that in the hospital, by no one.

Ndongo Passy and Grekpoubou left together. They went to the *Phénicia* cafe and ordered two nice, cold juices.

'I've already paid Catherine some of her fee, sister. We're so lucky Lidou hid that money in his office!'

They laughed, remembering the night they'd broken the doors down to help themselves before the thieving Zouaboua could. Because they were in the centre of town, they decided to go to the market for some provisions; one chose smoked meat, the other two large smoked fish.

The dry days of May went by and Mothers' Day came around. Men dressed as women, forgot to hit their wives that day and prepared the family meal. Gbandagba gave Ndongo Passy a pearl bracelet he'd made for her himself. Grekpoubou was showered with kisses by her son and her daughters. Catherine, not yet a mother herself, phoned Ndongo Passy to remind her that tomorrow was the big day and it was important to be at court on time. She added, 'You're a mother, Ndongo Passy, so Happy Mothers' Day.'

'Thank you, but really, Mothers' Day is worse than

Independence Day.'

'Yes.'

'Does the president celebrate this day with his wife? Does he dress as a woman and prepare the *ngoundja* after he's been to the market?'

'I don't think so. The president isn't like other men.'

The day after Mothers' Day, the co-widows found themselves back in the court room, Jean de Dieu beside them.

'Hopefully, in our own lives anyway, this day can be the day we celebrate 'Widows' Day,' said Ndongo Passy.

Zouaboua, Songowali and some of the family's other thieves sat in the middle of the room. Their large lawyer was exchanging pleasantries with Catherine. The co-widows and Jean de Dieu sat towards the back. Soon the room was almost full.

The case of the co-widows versus Zouaboua was the first on the agenda for the day. The lawyers approached the judge side by side to hear the judgement. Inside, the fans whirred; outside, the world continued to turn on its axis and around the sun, as if everything was the same as ever. The judge, whose voice was weaker than a Gbazabangui Fauves fan's immediately after a match, announced, 'The court declares that the bla bla bla of the co-widows of the late Lidou, Ndongo Passy and Grekpoubou, is formally admissible bla bla bla... but the court bla bla bla... dismisses it on its substance bla bla bla... because the complaint is ill-founded bla bla blaaah...'

He went on, speaking as if his words were neutral and were not crushing human lives; as if he was choosing whether to side with a snake against a rat or decide between a papaya and a mango for most beautiful fruit of the year. Ndongo Passy went rigid. She stared straight ahead without seeing anything. Grekpoubou took a little while to understand that they'd lost, that the judge sitting in front of her with the funny hat on his head had decided in favour of the liars.

Catherine walked outside with the women. Jean de Dieu followed them in silence. No one noticed the man in the black and yellow robe, with the Fulani hat on his head, not far behind them. The co-widows and Catherine stopped once more underneath the CNLC poster. Catherine said seriously, 'I'm sorry, I lost your case, but it's not over, and...'

'It's over.'

'But...'

'It's over.'

'I understand now,' said Ndongo Passy. 'This is not a case of guardian spirit *yandas* from the great forest coming to support Zouaboua. It's just *pété goro,* simple bribery. The judge of Justice, the judge they say is impartial, he was bought, the way you can buy kola or groundnuts.'

Catherine looked at Ndongo Passy as if she'd never seen her before. This neighbourhood woman who'd barely been to school, who would be incapable of telling you whether the Amazon covered the North Pole, the South Pole or some other part of the planet, had eyes and ears to see and understand life in Bangui. She'd never read the Declaration Of Human Rights or the *Kouroukan Fouga*, but she was a shrewd observer of day to day deeds and words.

'You're right,' said Catherine, 'A lawyer can't perform miracles unless they're willing and able to bribe a judge.'

They arranged a meeting for the next week. Jean de Dieu hadn't opened his mouth. As someone who went to court nearly every day, he knew only too well that his country's justice system was like a computer infected with a thousand viruses, and that the anti-virus treatment promised at every election continued to be a long time coming.

'Hello Madame.'

Ndongo Passy took in the tall Fulani man standing in front of her in the bright sunlight, his hat in his hand.

'You're Lidou's wife?'

'Yes… his widow.'

'I only learned of Lidou's death during the trial. It's a long time since I saw him. I thought he was travelling. He was supposed to do a job for me, a dairy shed for my cattle.'

'He's not building anything any more. He's left me, and my son.'

'I know. I was at the trial. I've been there since the first day. I had a trial of my own going on at the same time. Well, I must go now. But where do you live?'

'At the moment I'm in PK 26. I went back to my parents' house.'

The man took out a 10,000 franc note and offered it to Ndongo Passy. 'For the taxi,' he said, then added, 'We could see each other, later. If you need anything, here's my card.'

He turned on his heel and left. Ndongo Passy read:

Imoussa Yamssa

Stock Breeder
New Big Farm

PK 13, Boali road

tel: 76 22 25 37
email: imyamssa@yahoo.fr

'Did you see that, Grekpoubou? That man knew our husband. He gave me ten thousand francs for travel! Here's five thousand for you.'

Grekpoubou took the money.

'I'll see you tomorrow. I'll divide up the notes that are left from Lidou's treasure. Half for you, half for me.'

The widows embraced, as they had every time they'd separated since the death of their husband. Each took a taxi. Mangoes that seemed to have fallen from the sky covered the road, perhaps trying to plug the holes that gnawed away at the tarmac bit by bit every year.

Did the co-widows think the same thing at the same time, do the same thing at the same time, even though they were apart, the way twins do? Certainly on this particular occasion, when they each got home, one to Ouango, the other to PK 26, Damara road, they undid their braids and washed their heads. Washing your head can't wipe away bad thoughts, those that cause the most damage, but perhaps the hot water, the cold water, the caress of your fingertips on your scalp, can stimulate life, encourage it to continue.

Ndongo Passy's elderly mother tried to cheer her daughter up with kind words. Ndongo Passy soothed her, 'We lost. That's the way life is for widows. In this country widows spend their entire lives being ill-treated. But my life will carry on, Mother. Beyond the next village there's always another.'

10

A Fulani is a Fulani, whether he was born in Fouta-Djalon, near the Malinkes and the Soussous, or with the Bantus next to the huge forests that still shelter Pygmies. The Fulani is as black as a Bantu, but still drinks as much white milk today as his father's grandfather's great-grandfather did. People say the Fulani are beautiful people, and it's true. They also say the Bororos are the most beautiful of all the Fulanis. That's one opinion. All Fulanis or Bantus are men like any others, walking the same earth: the father first sees ants before his son does, and he doesn't know if water's hot or cold until he touches it.

Imoussa Yamssa, known to everyone in PK 13 as Ssassa, measured the passing of time by the size of his herds: if a Fulani man can count his oxen, he knows his age. Imoussa knew exactly how many horned oxen, how many sheep, how

many goats and how many laying hens he'd had at the time
his wife Sarang died. He could read and write, and for a while
had been noting down important events in his life in a bank
diary. The birth of a heifer, or his meeting with Ndongo Passy,
or his purchase of a new four-door Suzuki 4x4 from CFAO
Motors (white like milk, the milk of mothers, cows and sheep).
Imoussa had had many years of schooling; he knew the world.
He knew that all mothers, black and white, had white milk and
red blood.

He drove carefully. A new 4x4 had to be acclimatised
to, just as a new wife did; there was no point rushing. He
arrived at PK 12 and took a left at the roundabout towards
Damara. The new road offered pretty much the same view as
the previous one: more pedestrians than vehicles; motorbikes,
bicycles and ancient, overloaded bush taxis racing each other.
If the minister for public works had been serious about his job,
he'd have placed a sign every 100 metres that read 'warning,
danger of death'.

A group of military men were training, running along the
road in single file. As Imoussa drew level with them, he heard
their chanting, and recognised some of the words:

> *ya ya hé hé hé ya ya hé... balota a pika ngaba hé hé
> hé...*
> *mama a tô yein mama a tô ngoundja na yein ?*
> *Ngoundja na ngoundja.*

He didn't hear the next part, but he knew it, as everyone did:

> *mama a tô yein mama a tô ngoundja, ngoundja na*

yeinngoundja na korobo korobo ti zoua korobo ti bagara[2]

Oh yes, the part about the ox testicles was familiar to him.

His own oxen troupe was even larger than this military one: he'd soon have more oxen than there were trees in the forest. Everything on an ox has a use, even their horns: when they no longer point their sharp ends towards the sky as the animal grazes, they can be turned into musical instruments, or cups for drinking *kangoya*. Yamssa was a Muslim, though; he used his cups only for water or juice.

He sounded his horn at least a hundred times to clear the road of the peddlers transporting meat, firewood and charcoal into town. White manioc and black charcoal: a mix for a mestizo life.

At PK 26, he addressed a woman selling *nguènguè* fish by the roadside.

'Excuse me, Madam. I'm looking for a widow. She's just arrived here. Her name is Ndongo Passy.'

'I don't know her. Go and ask that man who's stopped next to the red motorbike over there.'

Fifty metres further on, Yamssa repeated his question to a man who had his head hidden under a large cap, his eyes behind sunglasses. He wore a T-shirt with a heart and the letters 'NY'. Perhaps he was also acquainted with Harlem and the Bronx, but he'd certainly grown up locally, for he answered Yamssa without hesitation, 'Follow me. I know

---

[2] With a hundred and fifty francs, you can get yourself a wife. What has mother prepared? Manioc leaves. Mother has prepared manioc leaves, with testicles of what? Mother has prepared manioc leaves, with testicles of ox.

where she is. I know her and her parents.'

Yamssa drove behind the man on the motorbike off the main road, to a compound half-concealed by a tall, broad-leaved beechwood tree. He parked, stepped out of his 4x4 and placed his hat on his head.

He saw Ndongo Passy as soon as he entered the courtyard. She was preparing *gozo*, gradually sliding flour into boiling water from a large gourd. He watched for a moment and felt the same way he had the first time he'd seen her, in the courtroom. He thought again, 'It's as if she doesn't have an age. She's neither young nor old, she's herself. She's completely unlike anyone else.'

He stepped into her line of sight. Ndongo Passy had already sensed a presence. She raised her head and they greeted each other with a simple hello, behind which Yamssa concealed his feelings, Ndongo Passy her surprise.

'Yamssa, where are you heading?'

'Nowhere. Here. I came to see you.'

'Sit down, then.'

She indicated a small bench in the shade. 'I'm just cooking, I'll be with you in a minute. Would you like some water?'

She called her mother, who brought a large glass of cold water. A moment later, when he'd finished his drink, she brought her stool and sat beside him.

'Why are you here, Yamssa?'

'I came to see you, and to see my friend Lidou's child. It's the holidays, isn't it?'

'Yes, the children are off school all week.'

'How's your life here, Ndongo Passy?'

In few words at first, then a few more, she told him. When

he mentioned the trial, she said, 'We lost, but that's life. Life's a chameleon; always changing colour.'

'I lost my court case too.'

She gave him a questioning look. He continued, 'My oxen destroyed some fields of manioc and yam. I paid a hundred thousand francs in damages. But the farmers kept asking for more and more. I refused, so I was summoned before the judge. That's what I was doing there that day. I'm a Fulani, a Bororo. Fulani oxen are always in the wrong. Did you know that?'

She responded by letting out a peal of laughter, something she hadn't done for a long time. 'Oxen are like widows, then!'

Yamssa spoke for nearly an hour to Ndongo Passy and Gbandagba, who described the new school in Gobongo where his mother had just enrolled him for the rest of the year.

Later that day, Ndongo Passy found herself staring at her fingertips after she'd moistened them and pressed them into the manioc flour. The indentations they'd made in the flour looked like a trail, an invitation to a journey. That night, before she fell asleep, her mind teemed with questions: 'Was I born with my fate imprinted in the tips of my fingers? Could someone read my fingertips and tell me all there is to know about me? Could Yamssa see my future in the tips of my fingers? Or even just by standing beside me with his eyes closed?' Ndongo Passy had lived long enough to know that some people saw what didn't yet exist and others simply saw the world as it was, and either cried about it or not.

Every morning Yamssa gave his orders for the day and made a tour of his land to check on the animals. Sometimes he had to cover several kilometres in the 4x4 to find all the shepherds and their herds. He touched the animals and spoke to them, in Pulaar or in Sango. He saw them as companions. Who else could he confide in, with his two grown-up sons at veterinary school in Cameroon and his wife Sarang gone somewhere far away, on the breath of the wind?

A week passed before his second visit to Ndongo Passy. This time he brought a bowl of butter and a bottle of milk, signature Fulani gifts, and already something of a declaration of love.

Ndongo Passy, who exchanged news with her co-widow every day, had told Grekpoubou all about Yamssa; his facial expressions, his gestures. Grekpoubou had said, 'He loves you. He wants to try you out!'

'But I've been a widow for less than a year!'

'So what? You're still young and beautiful.'

The adverts were right, it really was good to talk. The magic of the telephone meant that every time Yamssa left after a visit, Ndongo Passy could call her co-widow straightaway and describe what had happened. She also spoke a little of each visit to her elderly mother, who always repeated mischievously, 'Yes, I saw that, I saw that...'

Gbandagba, with the wisdom of his twelve years, sat thinking in his corner. He wasn't afraid of Yamssa. The man had the right to love his mother. He knew the days could run away with themselves until everyone had grown up and grown old and still nothing would take his mother away from him. Ndongo Passy had always been his only mother, even when they lived with Lidou and Grekpoubou had been another mother under the same roof. Like most mothers, Ndongo Passy had breast-fed her son, and the milk she'd given him up until the age of eighteen months was a stronger bond between them than the traditional *mbuki* that some people still practised to seal promises with blood.

One Friday morning, Yamssa paid a visit to Ndongo Passy at PK 26. This time, as well as the bowl of butter and the bottle of milk he always brought, he presented a heavy cut of beef wrapped in a white sheet that had been stained red.

'It's good, fresh meat, Ndongo Passy. It's still bleeding a bit. It's for you and your child and your family.'

He didn't stay that time; he had to hurry to get back for the midday prayer.

'Grekpoubou, can you hear me?'

'Of course I can, I'm answering aren't I?'

'I'm coming, I'm getting in a taxi right now. I'm bringing you meat. Lots of it.'

'What? Is there game on the Damara road just now?'

'No, it's from Yamssa.'

A little later the same morning, as Grekpoubou thanked Ndongo Passy for the three kilos of good meat, she observed simply, 'Yes, that Yamssa would make a good husband.'

Ndongo Passy burst out laughing. She had definitively re-discovered her *joie de vivre*. 'But sister,' she joked, 'Is a good husband no more than a good giver of meat? Surely he should also know how to make love lovingly and never pick a fight?'

'Oh yes, but Yamssa will know all about that.'

'About what?'

'The love part. Don't you think?'

Before going to his morning class, Gbandagba had got into the habit of eating a breakfast of milk and bread with butter and honey. No more leftovers of *gozo* or porridge for him! One morning, waiting for the bus to school, he noticed Yamssa's white 4x4 and smiled: his supplies of milk and butter were arriving.

Ndongo Passy smiled too when she saw Yamssa. His visits had become regular, and the brief moments they shared, whether speaking or silent, brought her great happiness.

'*Salam aleykoum.*'

'*Aleykoum salam.*'

It was she who had chosen to greet him using those words, to honour his faith. He placed his offerings of milk and butter on the ground at her feet, as he always did; they exchanged some small talk, as they always did; and when they spoke, as always, the simple words that came from their mouths seemed to weave together and become something else, something more beautiful, more solid and more sweet. Then Yamssa said, 'Ndongo Passy, on Saturday I'm receiving guests at my home. They're going to buy a lot of my oxen. They do it every year, they take them to Cameroon and re-sell the meat there. I give them an evening meal. Meat and bananas.'

'Ah.'

'The Fulani also likes fish, Ndongo Passy. If it's well-cooked.'

'Is that so?'

'It is.'

'The Fulani isn't afraid a fish bone might pierce his tongue?'

'The Fulani is brave; he can take on fish bones!'

'Hmm.'

'You know I lost my wife, Ndongo Passy. She was the

only wife I had.'

'Yes, you told me.'

'Come to my house on Saturday. My cook will prepare the meat in milk, and you can prepare the fish. With leaves, or with rice, however you want to.'

Ndongo Passy's heart began to beat a little more quickly. Her tongue felt dry in her mouth. She took a moment to re-adjust her headscarf over her hair before replying, 'Hmmm… I could. But what if I don't prepare the fish well?'

'You'll prepare it very well. You know that.'

He got up and placed a bundle of notes on Ndongo Passy's knee. 'Here are some ten thousand notes for the fish and the sauce and the taxi.'

'All right. I'll come with my co-widow. She'll help with the cooking. How many people is it for?'

'Twelve or fifteen.'

'Then I hope you have plenty of large pots.'

11

Tomatoes, aubergines, onions, garlic, parsley, bay leaves, thyme, oil, stock cubes. It was as if they were ransacking the market. They gave it all to Grekpoubou's eldest daughter Ibenga to carry – she'd been commandeered to help for the whole day.

They made their way to the fish, walking past the smoked fish straight to the stalls selling large *kpétés*. They chose five of those and agreed on a price. After that they bought an *mbossi*, another fish that had few bones, and headed towards the plantain stalls.

'Is that everything, sister? Have we forgotten anything?'

'Maybe a bit of ginger.'

'Oh yes. All men need a bit of ginger. It cures backache, doesn't it?'

They filled the boot of a taxi with their purchases and

all three set off for Yamssa's place at PK 13, Ngola, via the bakers. The radio played *Logobi danse*, sung of course by Logobi. The tune's syncopated beat seemed to provoke their driver to speed up. Grekpoubou, who'd been sensing tension from her co-widow for some time, asked, 'Sister, is this going to be OK?'

'Yes...'

'So why are you sitting there all stiff?'

'You know it's been a long time since I prepared food for a man, Grekpoubou. It's not easy.'

'Why not?'

'When you offer a man a meal you've cooked, it's like showing yourself naked.'

'Don't talk crazy!'

'When you cook you show who you really are. It's the same.'

'You're exaggerating, sister!'

Yamssa's house was a surprise. It was large and very beautiful, with a huge terrace, surrounded by shady trees. The co-widows were met by the cook. He was alone. Yamssa had gone out with his guests, no doubt to see the oxen.

The cook didn't make friendly conversation; he just took the co-wives straight to the kitchen and began to point out its impressive features, which included a cooker with four gas burners as well as two electric rings. He didn't explain where the generator that powered all those things was.

'Brother,' said Ndongo Passy, 'Do you see that umbrella tree in the garden?'

'Yes.'

'That's where we're going to cook. Get someone to bring us some firewood, three pots bigger than your head and some stones for making two hearths.'

'But...'

'Shhh. We're women. We know how to cook. You do it in your closed kitchen, we'll do it in our outdoor kitchen.'

The cook clearly liked to present himself as even fancier than the whites, but he could see there was no point playing the grand chef with Ndongo Passy. As he turned away, she shouted after him, 'And some salt, we forgot to bring salt!'

After a while, two young women appeared. One pushed a wheelbarrow containing six large stones for the hearth as well as two small benches. The other held the salt, and had a basket of wood on her back. Ndongo Passy spoke with them for a while. They did everything at the house: cleaning, washing, going to the market. Ndongo Passy asked them to bring a few other small items: two large knives, three wooden spoons and two small gourds.

They began, at a leisurely pace, to prepare their ingredients. Yamssa's compound really was immense, his house impressive.

'There's enough space here for four wives and twenty children!'

'Four, why not?'

They had plenty of time before the big evening meal. As they waited for the wood to heat to red-hot embers, they made themselves sandwiches. Grekpoubou sliced open three baguettes and spread them with ripe avocado and chopped onion. They ate hungrily. Ibenga sat on the ground, her back against the tree trunk. After they'd eaten, they got back to work.

The sun was still offering half of its rays to the world when the aroma of a fine sauce, then that of grilled meat with herbs, began to emerge from the closed kitchen in the house.

'Do you smell that, Ndongo Passy?'

'I do. That cook's trying to show off. What does he think it is escaping from his kitchen? Dior? Chanel? Citronella?'

From that moment, the competition had begun. The women were decided: their fish would be more praised than the meat.

As the sun began to dip closer to the horizon, there was a sound of engines, followed by a cloud of red dust. Three 4x4s entered the compound, fortunately at a walking pace, otherwise the dust would have added its flavour to the plantain, the rice, the fish and all the rest.

Several men and two women walked towards the house. Yamssa detached himself from the group and came towards the co-widows.

'Hello, everything all right?'

'Yes, fine.'

'You made the food out here?'

'Yes. It's better. Here we can look at the blue sky, chat with it, ask its advice.'

'Good. Well I'll go and have my shower, then we'll eat.'

'All right, but ask your housekeepers to come and see me, please.'

Yamssa left. Ndongo Passy said, 'They're all going to make themselves beautiful for the meal, sister. What about us?'

'You will be beautiful. I've got a surprise for you.'

Grekpoubou took a bright red top and a headscarf from her bag.

'You'll wear these to serve them. Believe me, they'll see nothing but you.'

Ndongo Passy embraced her co-widow. 'You've rescued me, Grekpoubou! Are you my co-widow or my mother?'

The two housekeepers appeared and Ndongo Passy gave her orders: 'I need two big, long platters, serving dishes, a plate for each person and four spoons, two for each dish.'

Three minutes later, she had the things she'd asked for. The housekeepers went to help the cook set up the tables on the terrace: two long tables on one side, two more opposite them. Closing the rectangle were two smaller tables on which they placed two lit storm lamps. The cook covered the tables with blue fabric like that used for *pagnes* and laid out glasses, bottles of juice and a cold water fountain.

The men arrived first, smelling of cologne, the two women not long after. All spoke Pulaar. Ndongo Passy observed this beau monde from a distance, in particular the women, who chattered to each other like parakeets. Grekpoubou, reading her co-widow's thoughts, said, 'Ndongo Passy, you're more beautiful than those two!'

'They're younger than me, I think.'

'Young? Can youth be eaten like a good plate of *ngoundja*?'

They placed rounds of fried plantain, still warm, on to the large plates, and arranged fillets of braised fish on top. They garnished the whole with slices of cucumber. Ibenga loaded each plate with rice, sauce and a good-sized piece of *mbossi*.

Ndongo Passy had laid everything out before the chef had brought the meat. She said, 'Eat up now. Those fish swam a long way before they were caught. You can taste their travels in their flesh.'

Everyone looked at her. She'd spoken in Sango, and it was in Sango that one of the guests asked Yamssa, 'Is this woman giving us fish or poetry?'

'Poetry. Let's eat.'

The evening was long. As night fell, one of the men sang a sweet, melancholic song. Ndongo Passy, Grekpoubou and Ibenga had remained in the background, eating their share of the fish and rice under their tree, by the light of their two hearths.

'Is that singer trying to make the stars cry?'

'Perhaps he's only trying to make himself cry.'

'Why would he do that?'

'Perhaps because he's sad. Perhaps because the one he loves left him for someone else.'

'Would a man cry about that?'

'I think he would.'

The guests were the first to go to their rooms. It was not yet midnight. Yamssa joined the women by the fire. He bowed and took Ndongo Passy's hand. She stood. He kept his hand in hers and they walked a few steps.

'It was a good meal, Ndongo Passy. You must stay here with me tonight.'

She let go of his hand. He added, 'Tonight you served my guests and me as a wife would. The fish was very good, the sauce was very good. I didn't even eat any of the meat!'

She let a moment pass before speaking.

'Yamssa, I'm not your wife. We spoke about the cooking,

but we never spoke about me sleeping here.'

He took her hand back again. 'Soon you'll be my wife, Ndongo Passy. Shall I ask your parents for your hand?'

'Yes, you could do that.'

Yamssa drove Ndongo Passy, Grekpoubou and Ibenga on empty roads through the night in the white Suzuki 4x4. When they arrived at PK 26, Yamssa murmured to Ndongo Passy, 'I'll see you tomorrow. Tomorrow.'

After they'd taken their shower, Ndongo Passy unrolled mats and they all lay down in the courtyard. It was hot.

'Are you asleep, Ndongo Passy?'

'Not yet. I'm thinking.'

'What are you thinking about?'

'A little idea.'

'What is it?'

'I'll tell you tomorrow. Or soon.'

Night passed and morning came. The moment she awoke, Ndongo Passy started thinking about the evening before. She wasn't sure whether it had been too short or too long.

12

Just one week, but so much had happened! Seven days, seven nights, seventh heaven.

Imoussa Yamssa was not a cattle breeder who had succeeded by chance. It wasn't magic that had made his herds increase more quickly than those of his neighbours. He was determined and precise, following through on even his most trivial decisions. Now he made calls to some friends and gave some instructions.

He knew there was no such thing as chance; that the Prophet – may the peace and blessings of Allah be upon him – had guided his life so that one day it would intersect with that of Ndongo Passy.

He'd sold twenty oxen at a good price. Later, after the evening meal, he'd taken Ndongo Passy's hand in his, felt the blood flowing in his veins, felt her life force merging with his own. He'd spoken the crucial words and her response had been apt. From the moment he'd first seen her, she'd seemed like a person who refused to let the world contaminate her, who navigated her life drawing strength and maturity from good and bad fortune alike.

Yamssa had loved and been loved before, but with Ndongo Passy he was a hopeful young man again, a man yet to make all the discoveries he was going to make with his loved one.

When he closed his eyes and thought of Ndongo Passy, he saw forests of giant trees. These trees resembled other trees, yet were nothing like them. Yamssa knew this without knowing why. These trees drew your attention; they were the ones the bees chose: in the hollows of their branches they made their honey.

Ndongo Passy was like other women, and also completely different. If you heard her described in simple words, you might imagine her just like her sisters, but she stood out from the herd, and Yamssa had found her. The words to describe those things about her that the eyes could only guess at had not been invented yet.

The Fulani are farmers: since ancient times they've left the prints of their feet and of their animals' hooves on the earth. They've walked from pasture to pasture, listening to the winds and breathing in the fragrances of the sky. Even now, when the world forgets to be beautiful at times, the Fulani remain poets. For the Fulani, words can provide powerful reasons to go on living and to love.

Yamssa wanted to pass through Ndongo Passy's eyes and speak directly to her mind, to tell her about the life that stretched out ahead of them. He wanted to take her far away, to a place where words, even words of love, were no longer necessary. He wanted them to set out together in search of delirium, to moan for each other and make each other moan, body pressed against body.

His steps, like those of his ancestors, had always taken him towards new horizons. Now all he wanted was for his steps to match hers.

Five men came, pointed Fulani hats in their hands, to see Ndongo Passy's elderly father. He showed them a bench and they sat. After a pause, one of the men said, 'Father, we are here to ask for the hand of your daughter, Ndongo Passy, on behalf of our brother, Imoussa Yamssa. He would like to marry her.'

The old man didn't answer straightaway. When he did, he first remarked on the sky and the beauty of the white clouds meandering across it. After that he gave his consent.

The men thanked him and accepted some water to quench their thirst. As they were saying their goodbyes, one of them slipped a banknote beneath the bottle of water, enough to pay for the old man's coffee or tea.

The Fulani got back into their car and headed towards Bimbo, to put the same question to Yalébanda, Ndongo Passy's aunt and the most influential woman in the family.

In the afternoon, Yamssa himself spoke for some time with Ndongo Passy's parents. As well as the bowl of butter and bottle of milk, he'd brought a young goat. As he took his leave, promising to return the next morning, Ndongo Passy followed him out to the road where his 4x4 was parked. He thought she'd come to say goodbye, but she said, 'Yamssa, there's one condition. Just a small one.'

'What is it?'

'I very much want to put on the wedding veil, to celebrate with you, to share your life. Your whole life. On one condition.'

'Tell me what it is.'

'My sister. My co-widow, Grekpoubou. She must come and live with us. I can't abandon her.'

Yamssa was silent. He closed his eyes for a moment. When he re-opened them, he asked softly, 'But why? I can't marry her too.'

'I know. That's not what I mean.'

She took a breath and explained, 'I can't marry and leave her living with her parents. They'll marry her to some relative as soon as they can, and her life will be over. If she lives with me, with me and you, there'll certainly be a better chance for her. She's young and beautiful.'

Before he could reply, she continued, 'I know what I'm saying. My sister mustn't be forgotten. Everything I eat, she must eat too.'

Yamssa leaned on his 4x4. The hat pushed down on his head concealed his eyes. This demand was unexpected, and for once he didn't know what to say. Ndongo Passy added, 'If you do this, Yamssa, if you take her in with us, I promise you won't get any less of me.'

Twenty days had passed since the sale of the oxen and the grand banquet. Day and night he'd been organising, giving orders like a rebel chief. He'd informed his clans-people close to home and those several frontiers away. He'd commandeered friends from near and far. He'd gathered the dowry for his future spouse and sent out more than a hundred invitations. The dowry ceremony would take place that Saturday at the house of Ndongo Passy's ancient aunt Yalébanda, who was delighted to be presiding over the celebration. She'd already hired the chairs and placed them in a circle in her courtyard, and her neighbours had begun preparing punches and sauces.

The entire neighbourhood was in a frenzy. Since the night before, pick-ups belonging to various tradesmen and taxis bearing gifts had been calling. There were *pagnes* of every colour, storm lanterns, pots, sheets, blankets, mobile phones, two widescreen TVs, twenty basins of sugar, coffee, manioc, and resting on a red and gold upholstered chair, a small box containing a million CAR francs.

And so there could be no doubt in anyone's mind about who this dowry had come from, Yamssa had had an ox brought to the compound door, its horns decorated with ribbons.

The co-widows, one soon to be a wife again, wore embroidered *pagne* dresses, one blue, the other yellow. Each had draped a light scarf around her head and neck. They looked like sisters. The guests began to arrive. No one could have said which of them was happier, Grekpoubou or her co-widow who was about to have a new husband.

Jean de Dieu and his wife were there. Catherine Maïgaro was there. Inside the house, Ndongo Passy and Grekpoubou were laughing, not for joy or with nerves, but about a little trick they'd played, the results of which they were hoping to see very soon.

Ndongo Passy, as ever, had masterminded the plan: to invite Zouaboua to the celebration, in his capacity as an important person, without him knowing exactly who was inviting him. They'd made a decorated card and had it printed in colour and delivered to him. This beautifully-produced and beautifully-deceitful missive said amongst other things, 'On the occasion of the dowry ceremony for his future wife, Imoussa Yamssa is honoured to invite Mr Zouaboua to join his family and several other important personalities for the celebration.'

The children of the co-widows wandered amongst the invited guests in the courtyard. Gbandagba and Koutia were wearing new blue jeans and tops bearing fake Lacoste crocodiles, and had red Converse Allstars on their feet. They looked a bit like doctors, wearing their catapults around their necks like stethoscopes. They came and went, welcoming the guests. They were the first to notice Zouaboua's car.

'What? Am I dreaming?'

'You're not dreaming, Gbandagba.'

Gbandagba made a decision. 'Koutia, go and hide behind that fabric. I won't be long.'

He ran off.

Yamssa walked into the courtyard. All eyes swivelled towards him. He wore a green *boubou* with gold embroidery. He couldn't have been more admired if he'd just that moment returned from *hajj*. Ndongo Passy and Grekpoubou watched from inside the house as he bowed before each of the guests.

'Sister, we'll wait one more minute, then we'll go and let ourselves be admired too. You follow me.'

They checked themselves in a large mirror.

'This mirror is like a guardian spirit. It makes us look younger and more beautiful.'

'Ndongo Passy, every time I look at you I know that for

years now you haven't aged a single bit.'

'Really? Is that possible?'

'Why not? And your marriage will make you even younger!'

Gbandagba came to find Koutia behind the cloths, armed with a large kitchen knife which could have cut the throat of a goat or sacrificed ten chickens.

'What's going on?'

'Follow me, Koutia.'

Zouaboua had entered the compound and was greeting all the people he didn't know. As soon as they were outside, Gbandagba led Koutia to Zouaboua's pick-up. He punctured its four tyres. As he pulled the knife blade out of the last tyre and listened to it hiss out its final breath, he muttered to himself, 'Nice work!' He turned to Koutia and said, 'That's not all.'

He opened the petrol tank and dropped in about fifteen sugar cubes. 'That,' he said, 'will make the motor cough until it pukes its guts up.'

They'd barely completed their commando action when they heard a burst of applause from the courtyard. Their mothers had come out of the house. All eyes were on them. Those of Yamssa showed pride and emotion. Zouaboua froze as still as a statue. He would have liked to scream with rage, but he couldn't move his mouth. He saw that he'd been tricked. He was in enemy territory, in the midst of the happiness of people he hated.

It took him half a minute to make his legs obey him, enough time for Ndongo Passy and Grekpoubou to flash him their loveliest smiles. Those smiles pierced him to the core. He withdrew, one step at a time, to the door, to the street, and back to his vehicle.

He was about to get in when he was hit on the head, once, then again: he'd been targeted by two masters of the 'special reprisals stethoscope.'

He climbed into the cab and started the ignition. The truck started, but stopped again twenty metres further on. He checked all around him, then got out. He saw at once what the problem was. Every tyre was flat.

'He got what he deserved this time, didn't he Gbandagba?'

'He did, Koutia. Everyone reaps the manioc he sows.'

'All was happiness in the courtyard. Playing along with tradition, the parents of the future wife were teasing Yamssa, dismissing the dowry as nothing at all, before concluding, 'Well, we'll accept it anyway, just to be polite.'

After everyone had admired and exclaimed over all the items of the dowry, the cocktails were served. The Fulani of Yamssa's extended family and his friends, the Gbandas of Ndongo Passy's family and the Yakomas of Grekpoubou's family all drank together, juice for some, beer or *kangoya* for others.

The Fulani retired first, following Yamssa. As they left, each one stroked the neck of the ox. Ndongo Passy and Grekpoubou were tired. They'd paraded themselves, spoken to everyone, been joint queens of the party.

Later that evening, when everyone else had left, the co-widows sat with aunt Yalébanda. The old lady was happy, telling stories about the time when she got her own dowry. She spoke of the husband she'd never loved, and of other men too, who'd touched her in very different ways.

Ndongo Passy and Grekpoubou spoke of the cruel and

venomous Zouaboua, and why they'd invited him along as a small act of revenge, so he could see with his own eyes that despite his lying and cheating, Lidou's widows were flourishing again.

13

He knew who his future wife was, the dowry had been handed over; Yamssa could, as the saying goes, lay down his mat in peace. But he remained busy, trying to get everything in the house ready. The room that would be his and Ndongo Passy's was finished, as was the large bedroom that had been allocated to Grekpoubou. The children's rooms would come later: the three girls and two boys would remain at Ouango and PK 26 for a little while, to finish their academic year at the same schools.

For the last two days, Yamssa had given his morning orders as usual, but had not gone to visit his herds. There was no time. He had to oversee the re-decoration of the large living room and the installation of the air-conditioning. He was having the generator changed too, to provide enough power for light and fresh air in every room.

For those in love, Friday, the day of Venus, is a good day.

For those who bow for their five daily prayers, it's a golden day. For those who eat no meat on that day, so have no need to go hunting, it's a happy day to enjoy a late sleep. The Friday of the marriage at the PK 13 mosque arrived. The bride avoided counting how many days had passed since the death of Lidou. Did it matter whether it was ten or a hundred or a thousand? A dead man was as dead after five minutes as he was when he'd been buried for 3,000 or 5,000 years. When a dead man entered the house of his ancestors, what had been tied to him was untied. His wife or his wives, whether he'd loved them or beaten them, were set free. So free in fact, that often nobody cared if they went to bed hungry. The family of the dead man would guzzle up everything they could: they'd eat the dead man himself if he tasted good enough.

That Friday was a good day, a day in need of no extra seasoning. The co-widows waited at Ndongo Passy's house, as inseparable as the two halves of a kola nut.

'Soon you might have another child, Ndongo Passy.'

'No, you know that's over for me now. It was just the one boy for me. I think I would've liked three boys and three girls, though.'

'You can still have them!'

'No.'

'You're young, sister! Yamssa will be able to give you them. You don't make a child alone. It didn't work with Lidou, but maybe it will work with Yamssa.'

'Hmm. What about you? It might be you having more children soon!'

'Me?'

'You'll soon have a new husband, young and pretty as

you are!'

'The most important thing is that we don't become widows again. People will think we're witches.'

The Friday midday prayer of *salat joumou'a* was over. The mosque was full. Everyone was waiting to witness the benediction of Yamssa's marriage; a whole room full of witnesses to add to the official ones, one for each spouse.

Yamssa's witness was a friend, another cattle breeder, who'd come back from Cameroon, where he'd fled after the Bozize rebellion in 2003, specially for the occasion. Ndongo Passy's was a Muslim neighbour from her old area. She'd chosen that person because she wanted the whole of her former neighbourhood to know that life could blossom again, that she was alive again.

In the stillness of the mosque, it was possible to believe that it was the Prophet himself – may the peace and blessings of Allah be upon him – who was reciting verse 21 of the thirtieth surah. Then the witnesses pronounced the ritual words:

'Zauwajtuka'
'Qabaltou'

A smiling Yamssa distributed kola nuts, biscuits and sweets, showered a rain of coins on the believers, then gracefully passed two bundles of crisp notes to the imam, for himself and his Quranic scholars.

Ndongo Passy would move to her new house straightaway. Yamssa had let all the servants go; he wanted to be alone with his wife.

They were not novice newly-weds, both had had spouses before, but they felt a childlike timidity when they found themselves alone, face to face, that evening. Neither tried to hide it: they understood that learning and taming the body of another is not a simple thing.

Ndongo Passy opened the door and the windows to let the air flow through the room: she wanted the wind to keep them company that night. She didn't want to hear the hum of the generator, so she lit just one storm lantern and placed it beside them.

In this low, dancing light, refreshed by the gentle draught of air, they guessed at more than they saw. They lay naked beside each other. He placed his hand on her stomach. They talked calmly, as if their night would last indefinitely, as if love had made them the masters of time.

'Ndongo Passy, do you know that in many ways men resemble animals?'

'Do they?'

'I think so. I know so.'

'How exactly?'

'They both need a place for water, a spring.'

All was still in the room. Tepid air slept in a corner, and on the mat at the base of the bed.

'You're my spring, Ndongo Passy.'

'Thank you.'

'I want to love you without stopping, to believe that you and I will never die.'

'You can do that. You can believe that.'

He put his head on the hollow below her shoulder and

left it there, without moving or speaking, for perhaps a short, or even a long time. Then he slid downwards and took the tip of one of her breasts in his mouth. She caressed his face. They could have stayed like that for a while, offering up the frontiers of their bodies one after the other to be caressed. But Ndongo Passy wanted to talk a little more with her mouth, even while she continued to speak with her hands, in response to Yamssa's hands.

'Are you listening?'

'I'm listening. Your whole body's speaking to me.'

'Listen.'

She held him close and went on, 'I'm the wife of a breeder now.'

'Yes.'

'So I want to be a breeder too.'

'What?'

'I want to be a breeder. Of chickens.'

He didn't move. He asked her to repeat herself. She repeated herself. He said, 'But that's no job for a woman.'

'Why not?'

After another moment of stroking and silence, he said, 'Why chickens. Why not goats?'

She smiled into the night and replied, 'For the eggs.'

'You like eggs?'

'Yes. Beyond like.'

'What do you mean, beyond like?'

She thought a little before clarifying her idea. It was not always easy to get the right words to materialise on her tongue. Finally she murmured, 'Listen well.'

'I'm listening well.'

'A fresh hen's egg is a very beautiful thing.'

'Hmm.'

'It's so beautiful, so well-made that it's like a testimony.'

'I don't understand.'

'Listen, Yamssa... I'm trying to say it properly, clearly... when a woman loves a man and a man loves a woman... they can live through moments of absolute love. Love so powerful that it's as if they've reached the end point of their desire. Do you know what I mean?'

'I do.'

'Those moments are the proof that God exists.'

'I never thought of it like that.'

'The beauty of the egg is like that. A complete beauty. Like those perfect moments of love.'

'Ndongo Passy.'

'I can keep talking. You can never stop looking at beauty, and you can never stop talking about it.'

'I think you will be a very good chicken breeder.'

He hesitated, then asked, 'When Grekpoubou comes to live here, will she be a chicken breeder too?'

'No! She has her Singer. She'll sew. That's what she likes to do.'

They were still holding each other close. Before the first light of day could surprise them, Yamssa said, 'Don't move, Ndongo Passy, don't ever move... I'm going to take you. Let my hands and my mouth and my body tell you a story.'

'Which story is it, Yamssa?

'It's a story that begins such a long, long time ago that no one can say what the weather was like that day...'

Glossary

Bamara a lango (*Lion d'or*): alcohol made in Cameroon, a mixture of coffee, rum and whisky.

Banyamuléngué: rebel from Congo.

Biani biani: for always.

Bili-bili: alcohol made from millet.

Boubou: a flowing robe worn by men.

EMCCA: Economic and Monetary Community of Central African States.

Gozo: manioc dumpling.

Kaba: very flowing traditional dress.

Kangoya: palm wine.

Kouroukan Fouga: the constitution of the Mali empire, created in 1235.

Kwa na Kwa: 'work, only work' in Sango. KNK was the name and official slogan of the party of President Bozize in the 2011 elections in CAR.

Linga: large traditional drum.

Maisons d'aujourd'hui: Homes for Today

Makako: monkey.

Makongo: caterpillar.

Mbossi: river fish.

Ndéké Luka: 'bird of chance'. Name of a radio station popular in Bangui.

Ngoundja: dish made of chopped manioc leaves, known elsewhere by the name of *saka saka*.

Nguèndè: traditional wooden chair.

Nguènguè: tiny white river fish, sometimes called 'little sardines'.

Pagne: a robe or skirt made of one piece of cloth wrapped around the body, also used to designate the brightly-coloured fabric.

Sango: national language of CAR, spoken all over the country.

Tromole: actually *Tramole*, pills said to give sexual muscle tone to men, called *Tromole* mockingly by women ('*trop molle*' = 'too soft').

Yabanda: dish of smoked fish and koko leaves.

Yanda: guardian spirit of the forest.

Yangbabolo: dance and the name of a well known group from Central African Republic

Zakawa: ethnic group in Chad and by extension, Chadian rebels who came to CAR in 2003.

Cover Image

Dedalus Africa

Under the editorship of Jethro Soutar and Yovanka Perdigão, Dedalus Africa seeks out high-quality fiction from all of Africa, including parts of Africa hitherto totally ignored by English-language publishers. Titles currently available are:

The Desert and the Drum – Mbarek Ould Beyrouk
Catalogue of a Private Life – Najwa Bin Shatwan
The Word Tree – Teolinda Gersão
The Madwoman of Serrano – Dina Salústio
The Ultimate Tragedy – Abdulai Silá
Our Musseque – José Luandino Vieira
Co-wives, Co-widows – Adrienne Yabouza

Forthcoming titles include:

Eddo's Souls – Stella Gaitano

For further details email: info@dedalusbooks.com